PERCIVAL DOOLEY

Percival Dooley

K.C. Foster

Percival Dooley

The Heights of Misfortune

by K.C. Foster

Percival Dooley: The Heights of Misfortune
by K.C. Foster
1st edition
Copyright © 2025
ISBN: 979-8-999-3695-0-5

This is a work of fiction. Although the story aligns with an actual historical period, names, characters, some places, and some events are products of the author's imagination. Any resemblance to actual persons, places, or situations is purely coincidental.

Printed in the United States of America

First Printing, 2026

Contents

Thanks, Mom, for always
asking me,
"When are you going to be done with that
book?"

1

The Heights of Something New

The story of the Dooley family contains suffering and soaring, in that order, so the falls held an attribute of hope, not dread.

Mathew and Lena Dooley followed their dreams from Ireland to America, settling in New York and finally Chicago. They had two boys whose dreams soared high as well: Reginald and Percival.

But Mathew never met his son, Percival.

Things fell.

Things such as Percival, for example. In 1928, sixteen-year-old Percival took a deep breath, prepared to fall again. He skimmed each foothold on each branch of the tree. He stretched to grab a branch, and he climbed. A black net around his shoulders tagged along as he climbed slowly with his eyes on the splotched blue bird. It didn't move, even when it had to have spotted him. Perhaps the bird wisely gauged its parameters for when it would fly away. Percival climbed higher. He balanced his feet and laid the netting's cloth handle in his hands atop his shoulders. With his eyes fixated, he flicked the net with a perfect snap of his wrists. The net touched the bird before the bird jolted. And in trying to maneuver his hands to trap the bird, he forgot to hold on. He stepped backward into the air, and his body dropped. The trunk and branches clawed at his skin. A low branch grabbed his legs and pounded his back to the ground. After taking a fall this time, Percival lay for a minute or more and wondered if his arms were attached, broken, or bleeding. He was still dizzy when a man's shadow grabbed him by his collar and forced Percival to stand.

"I said answer me! What's the matter with you! Answer me, kid!" the shadow growled. Percival grounded his feet as still as he was able and stared. The silhouette wore a fedora and a sort of thickness in respect. Percival said nothing. The man slapped Percival on the head, causing Percival to grit his teeth and grimace. The dizziness regained power.

"Kid," the man looked to his right and left, where only trees surrounded them. Few people traveled this road on the south side of Chicago. The man's coat lapel spun in Percival's head. Yet in the daze, Percival clinched a fist and soared it in front of him to the man's chest. The man grunted and grabbed Percival by the shoulders. The punch caused Percival to lose his balance.

"You okay? You're okay, kid. You're okay. But I'll leave ya' for dead! I'm just trying to help you. So answer me! Are you a Dooley, for the love of God!"

Percival stared at him a moment longer, unable to control the twitching muscles of his face. "Yeah. I'm Percy- Percival Dooley. What do you want?"

"Alright then. . . I'm Charlie. From the Blaughvoyon Hotel. You know, the big one. I'm here doing you and everybody else a favor, Percival Dooley . . .Well, I'll be hanged . . . Do you eat, kid? What do ya' eat? Clay? Are ya' one of those pathetic clay eaters? Go clean yourself up quick and get down to the hotel and sign up. Pathetic."

As Percival's wits returned, he managed, "What? I don't — what are you talking about?" through clinched teeth. He wiped his nose, smearing dirt and blood across his face and hand. "Sign up for what?" Percival then inspected his clothes. He was as clean as any, minus the bloody nose streaming down his neck and blotting his shirt collar from the tree fall. Charlie glared at Percival and shuffled his feet with a couple of intentional breaths.

Charlie started, "Let me make sure I got the right guy here. Your father, he's missing, gone. Out of your pathetic life, am I right?" He stared at Percival's face for a slight moment before answering himself, "Yeah, I'm right."

"So what? Who cares? What — you got a pap? Nobody's got one, so who cares?" Percival answered.

"Now, go clean up. Get down there to the Blaughvoyon Hotel. There's a new hire table. Write your name and home location — if ya' got one. You got a home?"

"New hire? You mean, like a job?" Percival asked.

"Yeah."

"You're giving me a job?" Percival asked again, feeling a soft breeze through the trees.

"What'd I say?"

"The Blaughvoyon! You mean it? And you say me Pap works there?"

"No, kid! And I don't need you asking me questions. What I know is if you don't get your pathetic bum down to that table, you'll never know nothing about your dear old pops."

"I don't wanna know nothin' about him. Who cares?"

"So you don't want the job? Fine by me. I tried." Charlie walked backwards a few steps.

"So, you'll pay me?" Percival stretched his voice with his eyes wide. "I want the job, Mister Charlie, but that's all. No family stuff."

"Sorry, kid. That's not an option. And I thought you were older. How old are ya', kid?"

"I'm … twenty-years-old," Percival suggested at the true age of sixteen.

"Sure you are. Maybe that'll work," Charlie smiled as he started down the road out of the forest. "Will ya' do me a favor and eat? And Dooley, keep your pathetic mouth shut about this. You speak, you find out nothing. Nothing. Everyone will go tight-lipped. You stay quiet, you'll find out everything. Capiche? Come to work and do what you're told." Charlie got into a car parked a few yards away.

Percival already had a job with his older brother, Rex. Three years ago, Rex created a bird-safety business involving a bird census program, traveling great lengths and climbing greater heights to tag birds. He sold tags with the purchaser's name on them, tagging their bird of choice – juncos, warblers, wrens, mourning doves, cardinals, anything with feathers that would be still or couldn't fly. Rex also received donations from bird lovers and girls. Critics and complainers toppled upon him, and funds dissipated. Birders scattered to new endeavors. But the brothers weren't settling for the business plummeting and a loss of their dreams to fame, to riches, to anywhere else. Anywhere else than Southwest Chicago; being in the midst of the wealthy at a posh hotel sounded like something.

2

The Heights of Chicago Life

On the morning of April 6, Percival awoke early to a thump, a fall by his mother, Lena Dooley.

"I'm alright!" she mumbled out. "Here at the table I just fell asleep. Your mum's tired is all. Percy?"

"Right here, Mum." He fought through the stench of alcohol and sweat permeating from Lena's plump skin and led her to her bed.

"I begin my new job today, Mum," he soothed out as she lay. She gargled something, and Percival left. A mix of nerves, high and low, ached in his chest. "Tis early morning. I need to leave soon."

"What new job, I said!" Lena sat up in bed and stretched a foot to the floor.

"My new job, Mum. At the Blaughvoyon Hotel. I'm going to wash me face," he tried.

"Are you lyin' to me, Percy!" rumbled Lena. Rex appeared in the doorway.

"You have a new job?" he asked Percival.

"I told you both already," Percival growled and grabbed the letter from the kitchen shelf. "I showed you this letter."

Rex took the letter from Percival's hand and opened it taut. He stood over his mum to read it:

> *Attention, Percival Dooley.*
>
> *Upon receipt of your applied request for employment at the Blaughvoyon Hotel in Chicago, Illinois, and after extensive calculation, we hereby offer acceptance and therefore order: you are to report for employment duty as an elevator attendant at 7:00 a.m., the 6th day of April, 1928.*
>
> *Upon arrival, the hotel guard will provide you with further instructions.*
>
> *Sincerely, Nicholas Blaughvoyon,*
> *Owner, Blaughvoyon Hotel*

"He's not lying, Mum," Rex explained. "But it can't be real, can it? A trap, I think."

"A trap? No! I really got a job!" Percival grabbed the letter back from Rex. He hadn't yet said anything to Rex about meeting Charlie. Why rouse up anything yet? It might be true; it might not. A trap sounded reasonable, but Percival dreamed of walking through the extravagant hotel, knowing the big-times and wearing a fancy coat and shiny shoes. It'd be his place, and it was a fancy Chicago hotel.

"What are ya' talking about! I'm sure it's real!" exclaimed Lean with a smile like no other. It was a pleasant smile to see, motherly and imperfect, full of empty spots and discolored teeth, framed with puffy cheeks. "Why, you're a dapper dandy, you are!" Percival sat a moment at the foot of his mum's bed and let her beam over him.

He applied for the job the day he met Charlie, and he didn't say a word about his pap. Why bother? Pap's absence was all Percival knew. Percival grew through friendships, fights, storms, and summers with no thought of a need for a father. He didn't look for him when he planned his thousands of days. He never knew him and didn't take the time nor the desire to change things.

But then, on some days, at rare moments, something opened a door of curiosity, of maybe. And it bled and spread in Percival's whims, reached his hopes, and even crafted scenarios that branched into new scenarios. It created a monster in Percival's head, from Pap dying in World War I to Pap living in cowardly filth in Chicago's wasted alleys. Maybe, just as maybes bleed, Pap was trying to find his way home.

The thought, *Who cares?* slammed shut those hemorrhaging curiosities. He didn't need his own messed-up reality getting messed up with more messes.

Percival walked outside to the neighborhood lavatory, and he couldn't help but smile. Rex made it outside before Percival, somehow, and stopped him.

"If it is a trap," Rex started quietly. He looked around and placed his arm around Percival's shoulders. "And me brother, maybe it's not. Maybe a famous man really wrote you a letter and wants to be chums. Maybe. But if it's not real, me dear poor Percy, fight like a wild Irishman. Want me to go with you, Percy?"

"No, I don't think so." Percival hoped a fight wouldn't happen. If someone witnessed him writing his name and address in front of the exclusive hotel, knowing he was out of his ranking, it may have roused anger. Rex wasn't way off this time, but it was another nuisance in Percival's head. Percival needed things, like money and a new surrounding, but not a pap and not a trap.

"You're not angry with me about the bird business?" asked Percival.

"What about it?" Rex asked.

"Well, now that I gotta another job."

"It's okay. You can work around your elevator hours."

An elevator attendant. This was new. Percival thought about it with a little hope and dread. If it wasn't a genuine letter for a new job, at least he'd escape a job involving heights.

Percival didn't fear heights, but the truth was they rarely worked in his favor. Heights were like a side-note he dragged along. To think that he wouldn't fall this time conflicted with reason. The most recent fall from the tree had left scabs that still splotched his skin.

All the changes were much to ponder: a new job, finding and avoiding his Pap, hiding this from his family, dealing with a fresh fear of heights — he planned to avoid any man who resembled himself. The hotel was big enough to do so.

Percival was as strong as any Irish boy from Chicago's Southside feral land, which was good. He rested his mind on the glamor far away from home, thinking he had a plan. Thinking he knew what to expect.

His home wasn't the slums exactly, but a step up to "rear housing." Lena herself considered the living conditions with pride. She kept herself and the boys out of the slums despite the impoverished conditions, despite the disappearance of her husband Mathew, despite her typical drunken stupor, and despite the neighborhood sharing a central lavatory.

Now, in the neighborhood's lavatory, Percival pulled a string for the light bulb and propped his mirror behind the faucet. He pooled water into his cupped hands and glanced at his reflection, full of shadows and two glistening eyes. It was a pleasant face the world erred to see as sunken and poor-like. He had firm muscles in his face that formed deflated cheeks. His facial muscles tensed and twitched.

The faucet water cracked into a thousand drops and smeared in a thousand directions onto Percival's face.

"Bua!" Percival boomed. The word exploded into fireworks with shiny droplets soaring in the air. For a second, Percival felt a lift. Percival's frail demeanor slid away as he watched his reflection. His head was still growing, perhaps. But for now, it looked rather scant. Still, he had a manly bone structure. Undeniably, it's no sap skull. His jaw, cheeks, temples, and brows defined their positions. He shaped his cracked, peeling lips in the same oval for both syllables.

"Bua!" Percival leaned close to the surface of the mirror. Feeling a little silly, he huffed out a small laugh. He was oblivious to how his baritone voice traveled throughout the dirt yard and to the hearing of early-rising children climbing and standing on roofs. They tried to mimic his low, thunderous voice with "Fool ya'!" or "Hoola!" as they danced. Members of the Dooley family were all graced with deep Irish voices.

Percival's apt to fall from great heights was not like his life at all. Percival should have been most confident that life would go on when he fell, not when he reached high.

3

The Heights in a
Different World

Percival's half-hour walk to the Blaughvoyon Hotel, a 56-floor gem in downtown Chicago, gave Percival time to think.

A new elevator attendant? He pondered as he walked with his hands in his pockets and his eyes shifting wide-eyed left to right, like they were looking for answers. Would he see his Pap today? How could he say nothing, like Charlie forewarned? He needed answers.

His thoughts of heights sped through his mind. If he truly had a job as such, then he was certain the elevation of being in an elevator — the heights — was the only thing to dread. He would fall because of the heights in some way, and that was the way it was. Where there was air between Percival's feet and the ground, there was a fall. That was the way it was.

But he'd rather have heights to dread rather than dreading the unknown of the day. Inevitable things like falling weren't as dreadful. It was more of a grumble about life to dread elevator heights than a foreboding dread.

The uncertainties of a foreboding dread were crueler on his nerves. If he didn't really have a job, he dreaded being put in his rightful place by foes — dread is worse when the future is fickle.

He didn't know what else to dread, not yet — but, to his own limited knowledge, it was certain to be a bloody fight or bone-breaking heights. As he walked, he concluded that either was fine was him. A smooth sea never made a good sailor.

Percival thought he knew the voyage, but the path ahead was as nebulous as his knowledge. Percival didn't know just how ruthless his near-future acquaintances would be. He certainly couldn't have known about the experience of another realm.

The Blaughvoyon Hotel contained a separate world, indeed. Not to be confused — this separate world — as *different* or *distinct.* It had something like a lifeline within another realm, as strange as it sounds. The hotel had a separate world. As many Irish travelers knew and experienced, most half-hour walks anywhere in *this* world had a tendency to arrive within the realm of another world. It's hard to believe until one tries it.

Percival made it to the hotel safely and uninterrupted. He approached the wrought-iron boundary that preceded the extravagant getaway. He made it this far, and his hope livened. The black rods of the railing worked as handlebars for those who stopped walking to stare, gape, and dream.

Percival approached a guard sitting by the gate. "Morning, sir," managed Percival. "I'm reporting for my first day of duty."

"Doubtful," answered the guard. "Name?"

"Percival Dooley." The muscles in Percival's face woke up with exhilaration when he spoke, and it caused his entire face to look enthused.

The hotel guard narrowed his eyes. "You're a kid. And Irish. There's plenty of factories in Southwest Chicago. So, run along." The guard's words seemed accurate but didn't shake Percival out of his dreamland.

"But, sir, I'm old enough to work — age twenty, sir, and I've a letter." The guard took the letter. Percival stood straighter and taller.

"From Mr. Blaughvoyon?... An elevator attendant?... Let me look ..." His fat finger skimmed a notebook. "Dooley, for the V. Nolan elevator? That's the fancy one!" The guard quickly noticed his own enlarged eyes and squinted them again.

"So, it's real! Yes sir," Percival answered, knowing nothing of elevators, but he kept a wide smile as he swallowed, shocked his name was included on the property of the Blaughvoyon Hotel.

Percival was rather small in stature for a sixteen-year-old, let alone a twenty-year-old. He kept his composure. The age lie was a lie he upheld, and he upheld it so well that he became pretty good at believing the lie of his age himself.

The guard cleared his throat. "You are to meet Mr. Hugenby in the Reading Room," the guard announced. "Straight through until you see books to your left. Straight through." He motioned a straight hand outward and repeated, "Straight, I say."

"Alright. Yes, sir," Percival responded. "To the Reading Room. Sir, any other jobs I can take besides being in an elevator?"

"Straight to the Reading Room."

"So, the library? Same thing?" inquired Percival. He was ready to hop and skip along the route. The guard stared at Percival and gave no answer. The truth of a job had to have meant the truth of Charlie's words. Percival turned toward the hotel courtyard and strolled into the exclusivity of luxury. It felt surreal one moment and brought apprehension the next.

Percival shook off his nagging nerves with each step between two rows of white stone beams which stood wider than live oak trees. Bold green foliage lounged immovably in perfect places. He continued under the arched entrance as if the hotel's façade either ate him or invited him. Time would tell.

His fedora, stolen for him by his hard-working mum, was slightly too small.

"It's perfect, Mum! Makes me head look bigger and older. Don't ya see?"

The long, rectangular courtyard stretched longer as he walked, so it seemed, and was aligned with several floors of balconies scattered with lounging guests. The dreadful thought of his Pap surfaced. Percival didn't want to see him.

Inside the core of the hotel, he slid off his fedora for a full view. A grand staircase welcomed him with a railing carved into wings and feathers in glowing gilt. The ceiling lights were encased in transparent gold jewels, and the air looked as if it was made of gold. The black floor shone so that the occupants looked as if they were walking on top of black liquid. The lobby — what a feast for the eyes, the hotel's golden smile! He caught himself mesmerized, and he quickly recomposed himself. Only children, not sixteen-year-olds and certainly not twenty-year-olds, lost composure.

Straight to the Reading Room, he repeated to himself. Would he ever arrive? There was still the parlor to see, the dining hall to see, a ballroom. Distinguished guests lounged around lit fireplaces, smoking early morning cigars. In walking past the variety of visual pleasantries for such a length of time, Percival daydreamed of having such a life. He held his hat. His light brown hair, styled and cut by a neighbor, pointed in every direction. The cracks on his lips seemed permanent; he'd had them for months. He was to meet with ... whom?

What the heck is a Reading Room? Why not call it a library? Must be the same thing, thought Percival, trying to pet his nerves.

A man in a dark blue uniform stood at the doorway of the Reading Room.

"Dooley?" he asked Percival. Percival's face twitched a quick smile to hear his name, giving him more confidence that the letter was real, really from Nicholas Blaughvoyon.

"Yeah, Percival Dooley," Percival answered.

"Knew it. Had to be you. You're the last to show up. Here," the man shoved a pile of folded clothes to Percival's chest. "How old are you, kid?"

"Twenty," Percival answered.

In the employee lavatory, Percival undressed from his white-collared shirt. It belonged to his father and was shared between Percival and Rex. Percival had sewn different buttons on it over the years. His brown wool pants were too hot for today, but they looked best with the collared shirt. He stared at the new uniform as he peeled off the rags he wore almost daily. His new uniform was starched without one wrinkle. The blue was a bold, dark, consistent color throughout. Tight seams of thread were taut and straight; Percival could barely see them. The uniform smelled fresher than anything he had ever worn. In the mirror, he admired himself. Its stiffness placed worth and character upon Percival, so he jumped and wriggled his feet in mirth. Smiling, he licked his fingers to lie down his hair. He waltzed out into the hallway feeling accepted and worthy enough to serve the cream of Chicago's guests. He continued to waltz down the hall. He *almost* looked sixteen and could rightly hope to pass for twenty. Could his father be close by? Percival glanced down the hallway before turning toward the Reading Room. With that glimpse, his life, though still young, completely changed.

A beautiful woman paused at the hallway's end. She wore a flowing light-gray dress with a dark green hat and a veil that guarded her delicate face and dark red lips. She struggled with a portmanteau and a suitcase. A large calico cat cradled at her chest in her left arm. Its old eyes sagged and spotted Percival. It suddenly pushed away and scurried into a blur and then to nothing, gone.

Perhaps Percival was in the hand—a grip—of the hotel now. If so, the hand carried the chivalrous Percival to the distressed damsel. Now only two feet away from the lovely masterpiece in motion, the air was lighter. And full, too. Full of Percival's adoration as he stood close to this woman. She had to have felt it. Percival stared at her, but she wouldn't look up at him; she kept her eyes either covered under the brim of her hat or looking down. The only women Percival ever saw this beautiful were in his neighbor's *Vanity Fair* magazines. He never thought he'd really see one.

"What, um. Wh- what. Uh, … lovely… day, Madam. Let me, um, help you?" his voice shook. His wide eyes could not deflate.

"No," replied the lady. "The cat—"

"May I help? I'll find your cat!"

As Percival prepared to sprint, she lifted her face a bit more, but carefully to hide her eyes. "Thank you, but no. Good day, sir." She dashed down the hall. Percival stood motionless as a jolt of something powerful filled him. He beamed.

He slowly found his way back into the reading room. His face looked longer with his eyes wide and his mouth open, his chin resting long. A slight corner of his lips lifted. He belonged somewhere.

Mr. Hugenby continued lecturing: "The Blaughvoyon Grand Hotel was built thirty-six years ago, in 1892, and it's the most prestigious hotel in the country- I dare say, the world!" Mr. Hugenby strolled from left to right staring into space as he spoke, with a cigarette in one hand and a whiskey in the other.

"Whiskey at six in the morning? Dudn't give nothin' about the Prohibition. What a guy, huh?" whispered Hubert Downey, standing next to Percival. Percival gave a quick nod and a smile of recognition, paying attention to the stances, the tilted heads, and the expressions of young men in their twenties.

"We are among the finest buildings in Chicago, and you men are our newest elevator attendants." Mr. Hugenby cleared his throat and met eyes with Percival. Mr. Hugenby paused.

"Your name?" Mr. Hugenby walked closer toward Percival and locked eyes. Percival froze and smiled bigger.

"What?" Percival stared back expressionless. "Oh, I am," he swallowed in hopes to ingest his wits back and answered, "Percival Dooley. Yes. Yes, sir. Percival Dooley."

"You were late, and you seem distraught, Mr. Dooley," replied Mr. Hugenby.

"I'm sorry, sir," Percival began, "but- a woman with arms loaded, and a cat—"

"A cat?"

Percival stood still as Mr. Hugenby stared at him and added, "Well, what happened?"

"Nothing, sir. It got away from her. I wanted to chase it for her!" Percival continued to smile softly with large eyes. He was certain the other new employees noticed his Irish accent.

"What?"

"A cat. A calico cat jumped out of her arms."

"From whom, Dooley?"

"This woman. She had this cat. A big cat. An old cat. I tried to help. She was walking through the hallway just out of this room, and her old cat jumped out of her arms. She wouldn't let me help her." Percival was still smiling, slowing down his words as if to remain in the moment. The rest of the group softly smiled with him.

Mr. Hugenby lowered and narrowed his eyebrows with a beady-eyed stare at Percival. "Where did she go?"

"Down the hallway, sir," Percival answered, pointing where the woman disappeared.

Mr. Hugenby pummeled the floor with his stocky legs outside the Reading Room door. He turned his entire body both left and right at the intersection. As he dashed back to Percival, he demanded, "Describe the woman!"

Percival inhaled to prepare to speak with smiling eyes and a smile resting on his cloud-like expression.

"Yes… I see," responded an understanding Mr. Hugenby. "Dooley,… her eyes met with yours, is that right?"

"She never looked up. I never saw 'em. They hid under her hat, the shy girl," Percival obliged Mr. Hugenby and chuckled, but he wondered why the man displayed such uptight curiosity. "Who was she, sir?" Percival asked. Percival didn't yet know the depth of the answer, how she was already part of his life.

4

The Heights of Confidentiality

Mr. Hugenby's face soured and swelled pink. He pulled at his collar, committed to finishing training. He didn't answer the question: *Who was she?*

As Mr. Hugenby lectured the group, he occasionally glanced at Percival, as if to confirm he hadn't fled — an annoyance to Percival, who scrunched his face with each stain of Mr. Hugenby's eyes. Hubert Downey noticed the connection with delight.

After a session, the new employees followed Mr. Hugenby down metal stairs to the bottom floor. He paused in front of an elevator and resumed his lecture on newer and older elevators, dos and don'ts for attendants, and answers to countless questions by Percival's fellow workers. Percival's mind was on several things, as a sixteen-year-old's mind would be, and little of it learned anything Mr. Hugenby taught. Percival didn't want to see his father, but Charlie told him something about having no option. He wanted to think about the beautiful lady he had met. He wanted to see her again and smile at her. Maybe kiss her.

The bottom floor lost the hotel's ambiance of luxury. Employees rushed in urgency through the hallways under glossy white lighting on the drab cement floor. Percival stayed close to Hubert. His eyes darted to every sight in the hallway. It wasn't so much that he wanted to see his Pap but to finish the moment and be done with it. At lunchtime, the new elevator attendants were excused to the workers' cafeteria for some hot gruel.

"Don't touch any other food you see in the kitchen. Go and enjoy. You've got twenty minutes.

"Not you, Percival Dooley," Mr. Hugenby leaned in and murmured, "you must follow me." Mr. Hugenby turned his back toward Percival and led the walk.

"Can I eat first?" asked Percival. No answer. Percival followed Mr. Hugenby.

"Are you kicking me out? Am I fired, sir?" asked Percival as he followed Mr. Hugenby. No answers were given. "Am I fired, sir?" Percival raised his voice. Mr. Hugenby continued forward with no answer. This moment was especially grave for Percival. Where were they going? Percival hoped it wasn't to meet his father. Perhaps to receive more information from Charlie. Percival hadn't seen him yet.

"Are you taking me to meet someone?" Percival asked.

Mr. Hugenby stopped and turned to Percival. "Yes, the hotel owner."

"You know me family, do ya'?"

"Heavens, no!" Mr. Hugenby chuckled as he continued walking. "Why? Should I?"

Percival and Mr. Hugenby gained access to prohibited entryways and traveled up to the twenty-fourth floor. Is this where troublemakers like the Irish were thrown off balconies? They walked through another hallway. Then another locked door. With access to a large waiting area, Mr. Hugenby commanded Percival to "wait here" as he disappeared behind a fourth locked door.

"Where am I?"

The brains of the hotel — Percival wrongfully imagined the knowledge thick in this place. A woman sat ten yards away behind a large wooden desk, the only other living soul in the room. Thick shoulder pads, thick wrinkles under her eyes, and a thin smile lifted on one side. Percival sank on one end of a dark green leather couch covered with buttons that tightened away any comfort. With a low, scratchy voice, the woman introduced herself as Luellen, and she stared at Percival. The desk lamp cast shadows under her blond bangs and shaded her eyes to look as if they had layers of secrets. She picked up her slim cigarette holder from the ashtray and held it fashionably, moving the shadow of smoke like a puppet.

"What am I doing here, missus?"

"I know you," Luellen sang. "You're Rex's little brother, aren't you?"

"Rex, yeah. Older than me, a little," he answered. He stared at the door. Who was behind there? Maybe Charlie. Maybe Pap. Percival breathed in deeply and noticed his angst. He breathed out a small laugh. "You're a friend of Rex's?"

"Once upon a time, in the sky, yes. The birds, ya' know. The 'Free on a Leash' program," she chuckled.

Percival nodded.

"Do you know why I'm here, why they brought me up here?" Percival inquired again.

"How is Rex? Tell him hello for me, will ya'?"

He stared at her a moment and agreed. She finally added, "Don't you know where you are? You're outside Mr. Nicholas Blaughvoyon's office. Button gave me this secretary job. You do know Mr. Blaughvoyon is the owner of this hotel? I've not yet even seen him! And he's building a second hotel presently. In France, I think. Funny, I thought he was there this week." She stared off and puffed her cigarette.

"Miss Luellen, do you know why I'm here?"

"How should I know? Did Button not tell you?"

"The button?"

Luellen blew smoke beside her. "Mr. Button Hugenby. He is the hotel's main hospitality manager. By the look of your uniform, you work for him."

After half an hour, Mr. Hugenby motioned for Percival to enter the room.

Inside the door and directly in front of Percival was an open space of nothing but marble floor and a wall of windows giving a mesmerizing view of Chicago life and Lake Michigan. Percival indulged his eyes out the windows. These were the kinds of views that switched off peripheral vision.

Mr. Hugenby's voice flipped it on again.

"Dooley!" huffed Mr. Hugenby.

Percival stood and gaped. Other than his blue uniform with the sweaty inner layer that stuck to his entire body like glue, this was what Percival wanted in life. Rich space and rich serenity. He soaked in the bliss, no matter the twitches in his face. It cradled him before the next unknown moment.

In the lounging room, Percival stood yards away from the hotel owner, Mr. Nicholas Blaughvoyon. A tall, slim, bald man with a narrow, long head adorned with a twirly mustache twirled in loops on each side. The man stood so tall and stretched; he looked as if he would levitate. Round sunglasses covered his eyes. Percival didn't recall ever seeing newspaper photographs of Mr. Blaughvoyon appearing so haunting. However, it was the height and depth of the man's long head that dripped apprehension into Percival, for it looked familiar. The head, that is. Perhaps from the newspaper. Perhaps from an old nightmare.

Where was Charlie? Percival was even curious to see his pap.

Mr. Hugenby fabricated a clearing of his throat.

"Good afternoon," Mr. Blaughvoyon motioned for Percival to sit on an extravagant yet uncomfortable couch as the hotel owner introduced himself. He stood behind a chair, apparently staring at Percival. By the roundness of his sunglasses, his stare was wide-eyed. Mr. Hugenby remained in the background. They towered over Percival as his chest tightened. Percival curtained his deep gasp with a placid face. The room had no other furniture besides the couch, a chair, a coffee table, and a rug.

"Um, I'm—" began Percival.

He then noticed a horseshoe hanging on the wall.

A horseshoe — he wasn't expecting that. A flood of nostalgia encased his mind. Percival's father, Mathew Dooley, believed in the Irish charm's good luck like a religion. Mrs. Lena Dooley told her sons, "Ya' Pap had it in his hands for Rex's birth!" Before leaving each day, she said her husband faithfully touched the horseshoe with the same simple chant:

"Wish me luck!"

Soon after the young family learned they were to have their second child, Mathew received a letter from Ireland concerning his mother's deathly illness. He was told to return to Ireland and claim the Dooley possessions before she passed:

They'll plunder away everything, the louses! Come claim what's yours, good man! Come quickly!

The letter offered hope for Mathew and his family to have a better life, to get out of poverty. He'd say goodbye, bury his mother, or however fate lay ahead, and get the inheritance. It wasn't much to pocket, but it was more than nothing. Yet, leaving his wife with child and a rambunctious ten-year-old boy rendered him reluctant.

"I must stay," he offered to his wife.

"Nah, me love! I can fare til ya' come back to me," Lena answered. "Just come back before he's born."

Mathew packed for Ireland. His son Percival would be born in six months, and he worried about the expanse between him and Lena, yet, as Mathew would, he glazed the sad moment romantically.

"Doubt thou the stars are fire,
Doubt that the sun doth move,
Doubt truth to be a liar,
But never doubt I love."

Shakespeare and a kiss bid him on his way, far away.

Lena kept a framed photo of her and Mathew smiling together, each holding the horseshoe when they first landed in America. The horseshoe hung on the wall until the day Mathew left.

Mr. Blaughvoyon interrupted Percival's thoughts, "I know. I know who you are, Mr. Dooley. Percival Dooley. You work for me." Mr. Blaughvoyon sat on the edge of the other chair and leaned in closer to Percival before he continued, "I heard a man named Herbert Hoover mention how dangerous it is to have complacence with evil."

"Yes, sir," agreed Percival. He looked around expecting his father to appear.

"You understand, Mr. Dooley?"

Percival didn't, but he expressed, "Interesting decoration--"

Mr. Blaughvoyon interrupted, "I can't allow evil to swarm its own fancy in my hotel and I not do anything."

"Evil what?"

"Any evil at all!"

Why was he talking about evil? What a torturous preamble before revealing the truth about his father. "Well, I'm not evil if that's what you're getting at! Everything they told me to do, I did it! I walked straight to the Reading Room, and I didn't do nothin." Percival managed out his defense.

"Well, I don't know you," answered Mr. Blaughvoyon. "You might be evil. Either way, I don't care, and it doesn't matter. I have a classified task for you, Percival," Mr. Blaughvoyon continued to lean close to Percival. "If you share even this meeting with anyone, including family, it will destroy the hotel and destroy you. Do you understand?"

This second new demand for silence was certainly a repeat of the first. These two men must not have known that Charlie already spoke with him.

"I know I have to stay quiet," Percival responded. "Please don't fire me today. I can keep my mouth shut."

Mr. Blaughvoyon looked confused, and Percival was glad to see it.

"Your word, for now, I will trust. I need your word of silence, Mr. Dooley. Do I have it?"

"I know. I can stay quiet. So, where is he?"

"Who?" asked Mr. Hugenby. Percival turned to see a genuinely bewildered expression and said nothing.

"Percival Dooley," Mr. Blaughvoyon began and then squared his face with Percival's face, "I–we need you… to catch… a ghost."

"Sir? A ghost, sir?" Percival asked. "What does this have to do with Pap?"

"Who?… Mr. Dooley, we need you to catch a ghost here in the hotel."

"A ghost?" Percival stood, unsure why. "I wasn't told about no ghost! A ghost?"

"Yes!" whispered Mr. Blaughvoyon's twirled mustache. "A ghost. Sit down."

"No sir. No sir," Percival tried to back up with the couch stopping him. Mr. Blaughvoyon stood as well.

"Percival, the task is simple."

"But I didn't agree to this. Nothing like this!"

"But we fear you're the only one who can help us. Please, Mr. Dooley, sit down."

Silence stagnated.

"I—what kind of ghost?" Percival asked as he lowered to his seat. "You—you don't mean—like a haunting? A demon? No, maybe— maybe an angel," Percival trailed into a whisper.

"This is a lot to take in. I understand."

Another pause of silence was now complemented by both men frozen from movement, staring at Percival.

"What am I to take in, sir?" Percival questioned.

"Disposal of the evil."

"Oh, yes sir," Percival answered, ignorant of the statement's veracity. Mr. Hugenby agreed, voicing murmurs. Mr. Blaughvoyon stood and paced the rug.

"But, sir," Percival chuckled, "there's no such thing as ghosts!" He smiled, hoping the men would as well.

"Percival Dooley, we have an evil in our hotel who cannot go unnoticed, and she must be squashed."

"No, it cannot! Squashed!" chimed Mr. Hugenby.

"Who?" asked Percival.

"Who?" echoed Mr. Blaughvoyon.

"You said 'she'?" Percival could not explain his questions nor even explain the moment at that moment. Nothing seemed palpable, as if he was stitched into a quilt of air. Where was reality? Was he a ghost? "Mr. Blaughvoyon, sir. Did you say evil? You want me to catch a- an evil ghost?"

"Mr. Dooley, understand this is a top-secret mission within the walls of this hotel, and it looks like you are our only hope." Mr. Blaughvoyon rang a bell from the coffee table. "If you allow this to leak, chaos will bleed throughout the hotel!"

"I can't catch a ghost! I've never done that! Is there training? Why me?"

Mr. Blaughvoyon and Mr. Hugenby exchanged a glance. Suddenly, a short man of Indian descent brought a tray with two cocktail drinks and mumbled as he walked into the room. He wore baggy beige pants, and he shuffled his feet as he walked. Mr. Blaughvoyon did not acknowledge the servant's incoherent audibility; he motioned for both Mr.

Hugenby and Percival to take a glass, none for himself. He sat back on the edge of his chair. Percival felt rather essential.

"How old are you, Mr. Dooley?"

"I'm twenty; I'm slow to showing me age." He was always honest about his Irish descent, unlike his age.

"It's my understanding you saw a woman today? With a cat?" asked Mr. Blaughvoyon.

"And he never saw her eyes," chimed in Mr. Hugenby, elongating his own eyes.

"Are you gonna tell me anything else?" Percival asked.

Mr. Blaughvoyon ignored his question. "Is this true? You never saw her eyes, or you don't remember her eyes?"

Perhaps he *did* see her eyes. He probably couldn't remember. Maybe he was delusional and there was no woman after all. He was trying to acclimate to a new job environment. And perhaps... if he didn't see a woman, he could leave this strange meeting.

But he remembered her wistfully. Thoughts of the beautiful woman placed Percival back in time, in truth.

"Mr. Percival Dooley, answer me!" Mr. Blaughvoyon shouted aggressively.

"Yes! No! I saw a woman, but I have seen lots of women in the hotel!" he exhaled all he had.

"Did you see her eyes!" Mr. Blaughvoyon's shout became louder.

"Yes! I mean no! Just her cat! I didn't see nobody's eyes!"

"Drink up. Now, down the drink." Without hesitation, Percival downed his drink, a lukewarm scotch. It burned his chest as if it was screaming a foreboding warning to Percival. Mr. Blaughvoyon continued, "No one has seen the woman's eyes. Few have ever seen her. She hides and remains a secret. Guests describe her wearing a hat with a veil, covering her face."

"Yes!" Percival agreed. "I mean, okay. I didn't see nobody wearing a green hat." The interrogation was growing to be nagging, and Percival wanted to go.

He did not say so, but Percival was certain the woman was no ghost; she was real, as in human with a living mortal body. She was a real, breathing entity. Percival was certain.

"She hardly ever appears. Never shows herself except in some unexplained disasters here in the hotel. Something horrible happens in the hotel. It's as if she's angry. She uses her dark powers," explained Mr. Blaughvoyon. He turned to lock Percival's eyes. "Something horrific is once again on its way."

"To me? Why?" asked Percival.

"I don't know, but very few have seen her. You're one of them," answered Mr. Blaughvoyon. "Catch her and your fear will be over."

"How do I- um," Percival realized this was actually exciting and fun, crazy. He couldn't hide a smirk. "How do I catch the ghost?"

"This is no game! You'll find yourself dead if you think so!" snapped Mr. Hugenby. Percival considered Mr. Hugenby's bushy mustache to be gross in his grimace.

"I'm sorry, sir and sir," Percival felt ready to confront this charade, "I never actually saw the woman you speak of. I just heard about it and was hoping to meet you if I—if I said I saw her. But I didn't. I'm terribly sorry and embarrassed."

"You never saw her?"

"Saw who? I mean, this whole ghost lady thing! I—I don't think I can be of help." Percival rose to hint of his upcoming departure, but not feeling confident the men believed his message.

"Sit down, Dooley!" shouted Mr. Blaughvoyon. "No one knows of this ghost. She stays hidden from everyone. Yet you saw her. Yes, you did! Why you? I don't understand."

Percival lowered back to his seat. Charlie never mentioned this part of the job. *Do as you're told!* Charlie said, but the instructions were vague and misleading.

Mr. Blaughvoyon shouted an order to his servant, who waddled out and picked up the empty glasses, mumbling more incoherent sounds, louder this time, and staring at Percival.

"Clearly *you* don't understand," Mr. Blaughvoyon enunciated with gritted teeth, shaking his head in anger. He slid his lanky body onto the couch beside Percival. "You have no choice. Your lies, your perspectives, they're of no use here! Please help the hotel! You have no choice," scathed Mr. Blaughvoyon. He paused and inhaled deeply with his head bowed as if he'd been defeated.

"Then, what do I do?" surrendered Percival.

"In the elevator is where your work will take place. You were assigned the V. Nolan elevator, correct?"

"Yes, yes. The elevator," Mr. Hugenby aired out the echo.

Mr. Blaughvoyon's legs looked long, folded at the knees as he sat on the edge of the couch. "When she gets on, close the door, close the gate, and don't open it until she knows she's trapped. Once she's trapped, she should die," continued Mr. Blaughvoyon. "She'll suffocate, I think, or become dormant. Away from the living realm. And that's it. It's that simple."

"She'll die?" repeated Percival. "She can't walk through the walls?" The two men stared at him with raised eyebrows.

"No, she can't move through solid surfaces. What she can do, however, — and be aware — she can appear in different forms—as a different woman, man, or child. I don't know how she does it! You'll need to know the hotel guests well. Know who's not a guest to know who's the ghost. This will take some strategy on your part. And you must tell no one!"

Percival wondered: how many secrets lurked in this hotel? How many more would he be ordered to keep quiet? Where was his father? Around the corner, or around the next corner. Coming through the door. Or he probably just walked out. Percival hoped Pap wouldn't walk in, but an odd time as now seemed a good one. Percival didn't know this would never happen; doorways would stay empty as he stared at them and waited. Mr. Hugenby and Mr. Blaughvoyon didn't mention Mathew Dooley, and they gave no indication of knowing this secret. The two men spoke to Percival as if he were twenty years old. He was now in charge of a heroic duty.

"But if I trap her, she won't try to hurt or kill me, will she?"

"Well, I don't know—" started Mr. Hugenby before being interrupted by Mr. Blaughvoyon.

"No, of course not!" he attested. "You may need to defend yourself, yes. Nonetheless, the entrapment will weaken her. Trapping a ghost—it overwhelms them." At the thought of weakening the woman, Percival frowned.

"She has you smitten. Hood-winked," Mr. Blaughvoyon stated. "She's not human. She's a monster. Your employment depends on satisfactory task completion. Catch the ghost. Trap the ghost. Kill the ghost! Save the hotel!"

Percival still didn't want to hurt her, much less kill her. He wanted to save her, to be of use. But he didn't have any experience in heroism. He didn't have the manly frame of a hero; he didn't have an American home nor an American family; he didn't have a father he could see, and he didn't have some other things which he knew nothing about. And perhaps if Percival had these things established as his normal life, he'd be a more likable character in this instance. Then again, without these things, he'd learn to be more content, happy with himself, but that didn't really happen either. He needed things to accomplish the task. What was the connection between staying tight-lipped about his father and secretly operating about a ghost-lady? Two powerful men relied on the young, impoverished Percival, and he was confused with himself. Why did he feel even less capable and confident? Percival, in his romantic nature, kept dreaming and planning despite the resistance of reality.

Percival, the hit man, planned to save her.

5

The Heights of
Transformation

The next morning, Percival remembered everything was different, and the ghost lady appeared in his waking thoughts. He stared at the oval brown stains on the wrinkled ceiling over his head.

"She wasn't a ghost; she was real," he whispered. She *was* a real damsel in distress, or she was a ghost. No, why would the hotel owner insist on something so ridiculous? A ghost? Percival felt embarrassed by his gullible responses, as if he were a child. Why did they taunt him so? What was their motive? No matter the answers, the lady — whose name he didn't hear mentioned — she was a human lady, obviously.

And he was now different. Everything was different now, except everything around him was the same. He'd be a different man walking into the Blaughvoyon Hotel today, where his father might be. His mum knew nothing. Rex knew nothing. But Percival had transformed, and they would surely notice something, something off.

Percival was again the first to arrive in the lavatory, escaping the slow waking of Lena and Rex. The wooden building settled in the center of the dirt yard and looked the same as yesterday. Low-standing, crooked houses cheek by jowl surrounded the wooden building. The familiar walkways still breathed away from the box homes where the broken sidings were still there. The stagnate smells and skinny children running on roofs — they were still there, too. Nothing changed alongside Percival. Nothing appeared affected by his transformation.

Permeating through the lavatory walls, Percival's voice shouted, *"Bua!"*

"Brew a? You're brewing the hooch? Is that what you're hollering about?" teased Agnes Wellington without a smile. Agnes, Percival's 15-year-old next-door neighbor, yawned and leaned her body on the doorway. With her strong English accent, she bothered, "You brew hooch with your mum and your brother, do you? I knew it."

"Nah," answered Percival, bent over the sink. "I said nothing about me Mum. Get outta here!"

"You're lying, Percy! Your mum came home quite loudly last night, like a true boozehound, I dare say. So I thought I heard you say just the same, truly." As he cracked a beginning smile, Percival lunged toward her with a pool of water cupped in his hands. Agnes jumped and sprinted away.

"Stupid girl!" Percival mumbled, once again, cupping more water into his hands. "Bua!" he claimed in a lowered voice. He breathed out a small laugh.

The dense houses formed a horseshoe wrapped around the lavatory. One side of their neighborhood, where the horseshoe opened, was a void space with patches of weeds and grass scattered around mud puddles and dirty, damp trash, but no homes. Percival thought of the horseshoe he had seen yesterday.

Five years ago, the horseshoe landscape prompted Lena Dooley, "It's providence! Meant to be, for sure." Two years later, Mrs. Wright, her daughter Agnes, and her new husband James Wright moved in three feet away.

Returning to his unchanged house, Percival worked his shoelaces outside the door, composing himself. A few feet away, James Wright sat on the gooey ground, gurgling and moaning away last night's drink. Percival looked in the window. His brother Rex, his mother, and Mrs. Wright sat drinking coffee. Percival let them be and opened the Wright door.

"Agnes, come help me with your smelly pap." Agnes didn't appear, so Percival left him and entered his own home. Lena, Rex, and Mrs. Wright glanced at him and back at each other.

"Why, a coal burner and a stove I see you have... Not... not common in South Chicago, now, is it?" Mrs. Wright's voice shook each word. She began humming in a trilled voice.

"Whatsa matter with it?" thundered Lena. "One for warmth, one for food. 'Tis what's needed in life, don't ya' think?" She stood over the stove, hollering over her shoulder with a batter for potato cakes and one hand on her hip.

"Among the rich, yes, of course, such as with my first husband. But here…" Mrs. Wright paused, shifted her eyes left and right, and sipped her coffee. She was dressed for work at the nearby nylon factory. She glanced at Percival, and defense raised his brows.

"After all," she continued and rolled her eyes back to Lena, "don't they perform the same expectations? Seems like … a waste, I dare say." Her voice trembled as if she were nervous to speak. She resumed humming.

"Me eldest Rex there found it for me. 'Twas no waste," answered Lena, giving her cakes a jolly toss of a flip.

"No, of course not, but I am afraid that … they say, you know," Mrs. Wright began, clearing her strained throat, "the Irish are adding things to their kitchens so they can—well, they say it's so that—and this is just what I've heard, of course…" Mrs. Wright takes a deep breath. "The extra is to have a still right in their own home. Right in their own kitchen, making their own liquor, I suppose. You know, to hide from the Prohibition laws of the land." She quickly hid her face behind another sip of coffee.

"What in the devil is that supposed to mean?" Lena roared and paused a moment to turn and wrinkle down her daring eyebrows towards Mrs. Wright. Without missing a beat, she turned back around and continued with her potato cakes.

"Well," Mrs. Wright started with a chuckle, "I don't know, Mrs. Dooley," her voice still trembled and shrieked, as if this futile conversation had a revolutionary meaning. "Aren't you Irish, though?"

"Mr. Wright is outside the door, Mrs. Wright. Passed out. Drunk," Percival finally stated.

"Leave 'em be, Percy!" shouted his mother. Mrs. Wright came out the door behind Percival and opened her own door for Percival to help Mr. Wright inside, wrongly assuming Percival wanted to help.

Percival pulled Mr. Wright by the shoulders of his coat, dragging him through the door.

"Don't drag him!" snapped Mrs. Wright. "You weak boy!" Percival pulled until Mr. Wright's shoes were in the doorway, and he let go. "Take his boots off, boy!"

"Agnes can," Percival answered.

"He's not my pap," Agnes answered.

"Ya' look just like 'em. You're sure?"

"You don't have a father either, but, of course… Irish paps, they always skip out. They're known for it," she said and glared at Percival.

"And you won't like what you see if you ever find him. Your father is wretched scum," chimed Mrs. Wright. Did she know? What did she know?

"Perhaps he's dead," said Agnes. Percival hoped he wasn't for the moment.

"No, he's not. I don't care, but he's not dead," argued Percival.

Mr. Wright's eyes opened. He rolled onto his belly and crawled his way to a chair in the corner.

"You should hope your father is dead!" snapped Mrs. Wright. "Better dead with a good heart than alive with his rotten heart."

"Like you then, Agnes!" Percival snapped. "And me rotten Pap, I suppose!" Mrs. Wright stared at Percival and gritted her front teeth. She walked slowly toward Percival before he was out the door.

"If he's still alive, boy, your mother will kill'm…. Probably just sit on him." Mrs. Wright pursed her lips and wriggled her head toward Agnes as Mrs. Wright waltzed out in front of Percival and back into the Dooley house.

Mr. Wright in the back corner heckled. Agnes smiled and laughed. Before he walked out the door, Percival glared at Agnes. She returned a placid look, and Percival sensed it to be a mask between her long, dry, frizzy yellow hair.

Back at the Dooley house, Rex rolled his deep and steady voice as Mrs. Wright sat at the table across from Rex, "Mrs. Wright." As if a smooth pouring fluid, he leaned back in the folding chair and protruded his neck as if to observe Mrs. Wright in depth. "Mrs. Wright," he repeated, head slighted, "Did Mum tell you? We're departing overseas to Ireland, Mum, me, and Brother Percy. It begs the question: do you want to go with us? With me? Get away from Mr. Wright and the devil girl?"

Mrs. Wright interjected, "I beg your pardon, Mr. Dooley! I am a married woman!" Mrs. Wright commenced her humming.

"Well, Mrs. Wright, you don't have to be," Rex softened a response. Rex learned years ago how his transparency shattered gals his age out of sorts, but older women didn't mind it. Rex believed they liked it.

Percival strolled as inconspicuously as he could toward the potato cakes. He proclaimed, "I began my new job yesterday."

"What happened at work, me boy?" Lena softly asked her son.

"What? Nothing! Wh- what?"

As he hoped she wouldn't connect his secrets to the Ireland journey, Lena said, "Ya raise enough money to leave soon and find ye Pap!" Lena smiled and flipped potato cakes. She took one from the stove, folded and wrapped it in paper and handed it to a staring and grimacing Percival. He tried to smile. Lena returned a puzzled look.

"Mrs. Dooley!" Mrs. Wright interrupted. "Your eldest son's lack of respect! What absolute vulgarity!" Her eyes darted back and forth from Lena to Rex. She edged on the brink of crying. This was something the Dooleys often witnessed from Mrs. Wright, but the brink never produced the fruit of tears. Mrs. Wright only remained on the brink; she wasn't one to waver beyond the brink; consequently, moments like this were why Dooleys didn't tend to those on brinks.

"Ah! Rex, shuttup!" shouted Lena as she stared at Percival and tended back to her potato cakes.

Rex interrupted, "Yes, Mum, but Mrs. Wright, do you love him?"

Lena, singing and bellowing, interrupted Rex, "To Ireland we go, Mrs. Wright! Soon now. We take a bus south, then east, … then northeast, then … to the harbor close to Ireland's western bay. We get on a boat."

"What boat?"

"One going across the ocean. A big one."

"Don't we need tickets?"

She ignored her sons and wailed her song again.

"Mrs. Wright, how could you love him?" tried Rex again over his mother's singing.

"Ah! Rex, married she is! Shut ya' mouth!" growled Lena.

"Yes," expressed Mrs. Wright. "Mrs. Dooley, when do you really plan to leave … the country? You know, Ireland is over-seas."

Percival tucked the paper-wrapped potato cake into his coat, catching Mrs. Wright's attention.

"Where are you now working, boy?" she asked.

"The Blaughvoyon Hotel."

Mrs. Wright spewed out a laugh. "Sure you do! Why, they'd never let an Irish boy in their doors, much less to work there. They must have you in the cellar, handling trash."

"I'm an elevator attendant," answered Percival.

"So fancy!" interrupted Lena. "He's a fancy doozy, this one is!"

"That has to be the most deplorable lie that boy has told yet," Mrs. Wright said and looked at Rex. "At least the boy dreams big."

"Are ya' lying, Percy!" Lena shouted.

"No! I started yesterday. I'm not lying! Mum, you saw the letter. Mr. Blaughvoyon signed it himself!" Percival felt normal for a moment, like he did yesterday, and he didn't like it.

Lena continued, "Meself and Mathew almost dined at the Blaughvoyon." Percival and Rex remembered the story: Mathew saved his crumbs of pennies for months to buy Lena a fancy enough dress to wear to the ritzy hotel for an elegant dinner. But after he bought the dress, he was broke again for such a long time that Mathew and Lena forgot the dinner plan and placed the dress in the hope chest.

With a quick goodbye bow toward Mrs. Wright and Rex and a dash of a hug to his mother, Percival dashed out of the home through the side door. He sighed with relief.

On Percival's way to work, he huffed out a small laugh and ambled through the maze between homes to the open road and open space of South Side, Chicago. As he walked, things became less cramped and less predictable and connected to more. More of what was hard to tell; the air looked bigger, and the buildings were bigger, but walking further into more led to tightness. He often wondered how Ireland would be different. More grass and more blue sky. Other Irish people who spoke poorly like him.

Puffs of Chicago steam and smoke did their job; giving their smoke no direction and no care to. He secured his fedora on his head and continued through the road's hovering gray air. He walked toward Lake Michigan, toward his new job, toward the hotel, and out of his own expectations.

6

The Heights of a Crash

During training, Percival remembered the previous night's dream — an avalanche, and he awoke just as the relentless white death touched the top of his head, just before it pushed him off the cliff's crag, where he, to the best of his memory, cooked potato cakes. What reminded him of his dream was even more frightful, for the event was no dream but Percival's present reality — the interior of the hotel screamed and shouted with a thunderous voice. It was a dreadful noise like a rushing train wobbling off tracks that became neither louder nor quieter but crashed into each of their unprepared nerves. The ground floor shook and was victim to the explosive boom. People screamed and shouted: "Earthquake!" or "War!" or "Ha, ha! It's the Union!"

Percival initially thought of the beautiful lady and of Mr. Blaughvoyon's words: *She's a monster!* In a panic, Percival and two other elevator attendants, Hubert Downy and Claude Mercier, rushed to follow Mr. Hugenby to the source. They stood panting in the dark pit at an elevator's resting place. Dense dust muddied their view. A collapsed rectangle looked thin and weak, scrambled on the floor. It had ingested a dark, wooded, mangled mess of scattered pieces; this frail box was entrusted with lives.

From the mangled elevator box lying just at their feet, their eyes shifted upward, and upward. They squinted their eyes to see the empty elevator shaft. It hid nothing, yet had nothing. They stood in either a sick part of the hotel or a wicked part. Perhaps both. Eyes sank downward again to see a million splinters of what seemed impossible to have all come from the elevator. The smashed box protruded everywhere.

Percival eyed a lifeless shoe attached to a leg in dark pants. The jumble hid the rest of the figure underneath. He quickly found other motionless parts of life—a bent elbow, hair, a set of curled fingers presumably on a hand, and an eye staring at him. Percival gasped and found that he couldn't speak. The eye then blinked at him. There was life.

"Alive?" Percival's voice squeaked. He swallowed and repeated, "He's alive!" People darted quickly with screams and shouts and bumped into one another. Medical rescuers quickly surrounded the scene, blocking others away. Mr. Hugenby stood a few feet away and spoke with a group of men outside the elevator room. He walked into the middle of the mutilation and stared a moment.

"Looks like your elevators don't work, Mr. Hugenby," shouted Hubert over the ruckus. "You really expect us to ride in these crappy boxes?"

"Training must continue," Mr. Hugenby stated, and he motioned for Percival, Hubert, and Claude to follow him down a hallway. He explained what caused the wreckage: A heavy oak armoire belonging to Mrs. Dawn Mercier, Claude's own mother, was placed on the elevator this morning. Mrs. Mercier insisted, against the movers' suggestions, that they deliver the armoire via the elevator. Fortunately, there was no room on the elevator for her to join the armoire. But two large men who helped Mrs. Mercier bring the armoire inside the hotel to place in her private room on the twelfth floor traveled with it and fell with it. The elevator climbed nine floors before disconnecting at a joint, snapping at a second one, and plummeting to the ground, as Mr. Hugenby explained.

Mr. Hugenby leaned in close to Percival and said, "Or so they say."

Despite the horrifying scene of disfigurement, training continued there on the ground floor.

"Are they dead?" asked Hubert.

"Just had the breath knocked out of 'em, we hope."

"And my mother is fine, you say?" asked Claude.

"She's in the lobby, quite angry, I was told," Mr. Hugenby answered. Claude exhaled words of gratitude. They walked on, pleased to go. The feeling of shock had yet to leave them.

"Reminds me of Emperor Nero of the Roman Empire," Mr. Hugenby began as if he were introducing Nero before the ruler himself waltzed in. "He used a model of an elevator in his own palace. A pulley, you see. No doors and no sides to his elevator, just a floor—my, my!" Mr. Hugenby shook his head with a smile, stopped walking, and lit a cigarette. His three students loyally paused behind him and exchanged concerned glances. He inhaled deeply, wiped his forehead with his handkerchief, and covered his forehead with his hand for a moment. Then he recomposed, led on the walk, and added, "The Roman model often—all of a sudden—would turn into a slide, and everyone would slide off. To their death, I suppose. Nero was known for such, indeed." Behind them were shouts and screams and cries of shock and exasperation; the sounds were Percival's nerves in audible form.

"And," Mr. Hugenby continued, "so are ghosts!"

"You got a ghost infestation in this hotel? I don't do ghosts!" Hubert emphasized.

Hubert and Claude looked confused by the statement. Percival kept his eyes peering in every direction, in pursuit of finding her; yet, in a sense, he hoped he wouldn't. He wasn't feeling firm in his footing. He huffed out some quick laughs and found himself to be frightened of her. Was she dangerous? Either way, he knew he had much to learn.

7

The Heights of a Cloud Burst

Along hallway echoed the scuffling shoes of Mr. Hugenby and the new elevator attendants. Long and straight ahead, the endpoint was a blur. It was a main, unseen, dark vein of the hotel. No one spoke as their minds undoubtedly swarmed with the horrific sights of the elevator crash. Mr. Hugenby stopped in front of an elevator located so far down the hallway it looked as though it were trying to hide inside the walls.

He slid the door open to reveal a black scissor-like gate and said, "By the looks of this elevator model, which wing do we now stand in?"

Silence. Percival felt a frigid chill in the hallway.

Mr. Hugenby answered before guessing surfaced, "South. The south wing. You must know where you are at all times." He slid open the gate, and with a gesture of his husky fingers, the three attendants exited the hallway into the elevator. Hubert mumbled some disapprovals. Mr. Hugenby ignored him. Percival noticed how the elevator didn't provide a safer feeling. From inside the elevator, Mr. Hugenby slid the door closed and then the gate. He slightly handled the lever, and the elevator whisked its occupants straight up.

"You must stop the elevator at each floor with precision. Flush with the floor—flush! — beyond this door. Not a hair higher! Not a hair lower!" taught Mr. Hugenby.

"It doesn't stop on its own? At each floor?"

"Not this model, no. You must stop it. It's part of your job!"

"Any other ... problems in history I–we need to be aware of, sir?" inquired the three attendants.

"Clearly, you understand if it doesn't work, the elevator simply doesn't stop, not peacefully, anyway. Why dwell on such dreadful 'what-iffers'?" He answered as he stopped the elevator and stepped off into the Floor 12 hallway. "For the next hour, you three are to get comfortable within these walls. Practice. Know the lever. Know your surroundings. Dooley, this elevator is like your V. Nolan," Mr. Hugenby explained as he stood on the safety of a motionless floor.

Claude slid shut the door and the gate, locking it shut, locking out the stare of Mr. Hugenby. He and Hubert quickly lit cigarettes and filled the empty air space with whiteness.

"Shall we go up, good fellows?" asked Claude between puffs.

"We gotta lose that guy. Big enough place to not have to see him every day, am I right?" Hubert said. "I don't care if he is my boss." Claude pushed over the lever. It lifted.

Silence.

"What if we don't work it right?" Percival said with a small laugh. He stared for an answer and lowered his eyes back down at the lever.

Silence.

"We die," expressed Hubert with a side smile.

Silence.

Percival swallowed down the shakes, and he had a right to wonder. Heights taunted him, and under his present circumstances, a mighty fall was plausible. Since boyhood, Percival had accumulated worst-case scenarios regarding heights. Lena admitted dropping the young baby more than once.

"Not me fault!" She shouted with laughter. "I needed three hands to raise ya', so I had to relieve one."

"Yet not relieve the other hand, Mum?" Rex and Percival inquired.

"No! It held me pint!" she'd shout with more laughter.

Percival also fell from an apartment window three floors up as a boy, breaking both ankles, a wrist, and a rib. A ladder mishap knocked his breath out. A prior apartment on the fifth floor meant either the indoor stairs or the metal fire-escape stairs attached to the building. Percival stumbled, bumped, and rolled down the steps quite a few times.

In his most epic height-related experience, six-year-old Percival accompanied seventeen-year-old Rex in cleaning windowsills of birds' nests at the Wrigley Building overlooking the Chicago River. Together on a scaffold, high in the air, Percival and Rex faced a large nest made of trash and feathers.

"Ah! Blasted warblers, I think," growled Rex. "Well, give me a hand, Percy." (Interestingly enough, this is where Rex's "Free on a Leash" idea was born.) Percival grabbed a bundle of the brown mess, and he felt a movement in his hands. A head with a pointy beak screamed at him. Percival screamed back. Startled, he jumped backward away from the bird. He fell at the edge of the scaffold.

"Percy!" cried Rex. The bird continued to squawk, ruffling its feathers after Percival. The young boy, in fright, found refuge in rolling away from it. His legs were stopped by the scaffold's post, but his body continued rolling. As he rolled over, the bird landed on his feet (which probably saved his life!). Percival kicked and kicked, kicking out and away from the bird, out and away from the scaffold, into the great wide open, over the Chicago River. For the first moment of detachment Percival was level with the scaffold but far away. He stretched his arms and legs, hoping to grasp something.

And then he fell. He heard Rex's cry — "Percy!" He sank through the air quickly, flinging his arms and legs. His body smacked on the surface of the Chicago River, which flowed swiftly after the previous night's torrent over Lake Michigan. Any other flow would have been stiff and solid, breaking all his falling bones. Instead, the swift flow rolled his body for a lighter smack and saved his life. Despite the broken ribs and detached elbow in the icy-cold water, a dock protruded nearby just under the first bridge with a small barge boat attached to its end. Percival was rescued.

A ripple effect of nature actually saved him. A cloudburst over Lake Michigan started it. Rain poured into the lake and swished into the Chicago River, deepening and speeding its flow. Birds of the area found a getaway on windowsills. One found a home on one of the Wrigley Building's windows; another bird found a home at a river crewman's bedroom window. It scratched and squawked and made such an annoyance that the river crewman woke up early for work and drove his boat that morning to the dock needing repairs.

It is arguable that the Wrigley's warbler caused the whole near-tragedy, but it's equally arguable that Percival was going to fall anyway, in some way. Everything was set in place hours before to save the falling boy's life, starting with a cloudburst.

After the regal fall, six-year-old Percival made the news and was known in the city for a few solid months. Chicagoans, amazed that a child survived such a fall, left the poor Dooley family with food, money, and pitied wonder.

Percival declared his bad luck, understandably, with heights. Yet Rex led him up trees during the Free on a Leash program. Determined not to fall, Percival's body scrubbed down tree trunks with tight grips to the bottom. He presently carried scabs and scars in selected places on his body from the day he met Charlie.

Presently, in the elevator, he still heard the memory of the elevator crash. He detached himself from the talks between Claude and Hubert about the tragic event. Their voices became a background blur. A small bite of his potato cake became an urgency. He pulled out his potato cake, made by his mother. Embarrassment layered over his nerves. He added some small chuckles. He spotted a crack between the edge of the elevator floor and the edge of the top floor's hallway. The latticed gate failed to veil this crack. What the crack exposed was the height at which Percival and his new friends floated upon. Their lives depended on the loyal clinches of the "automatic safety devices and double drums."

"Hey, you okay, pal?" asked Hubert. "You're making me all sorts of uneasy here."

"I'm not nervous. I'm okay." He smiled and huffed out a laugh again.

Perhaps mechanical perfection gave the elevator no choice but to be loyal. It had no choice but to work. He held his potato cake.

"No choice," he said aloud. Percival stepped closer to see more from the crack and felt a flutter of terror through his legs and toes. He huffed out another laugh. His colleagues stared and blew smoke directly toward him. Their attention angled toward Percival; naturally, so did their smoke. Hubert held an agitated expression, but not offensively; there was an understanding that this was his innate, God-given grimace. Claude was as thin as Percival, but taller. It was difficult to tell if he was naturally apathetic or choosing to be at the moment.

Hubert rotated the lever, slowing to a stop at the fourteenth floor. Percival unlocked the lattice gate and thrust it open. Yet, in doing so, he dropped his potato cake through the crack. He saw it slip and sink through, helplessly away from him.

He understood the fall. The terror of slipping through. Then, no foundation, no twelfth floor, no anchors, no guidance. Just emptiness to drown in. Four tall walls enclosing him, all too far away to help.

Down,

down ...

By the bottom of the tenth floor, numbness. He knew it.

Down,

down ...

But by the third floor, hope teased for a split second, perhaps hope for survival?

Down,

down ... before the inevitable doom terrorized again, like the first gasped on the twelfth floor.

And then nothing.

The potato cake lay still. He peered through the crack again and was certain he saw a white, motionless speck.

There was no crash landing of the potato cake, no boom. It was a fluffy potato cake. Mrs. Dooley crafted her potato cakes from her key ingredient being clouds; Percival was certain. Fluffy potato cakes warranted soft landings. And so did

Percival, considering he was still alive. Clearly, he'd keep going and survive, but the falling component of it nagged him.

The thought of fluffiness momentarily comforted Percival, but he refocused his endeavor to see the ghost lady.

He stepped out into the hallway for some invisible air. "I just need a moment," he explained as his coworkers agreed to put out their cigarettes.

At the hallway's intersection, a cat's calico tail hugged the wall's corner.

8

The Heights of a Ghost Hunt

The lady's cat? Percival followed the cat and turned down the hallway. There she was! In her dress and hat, she walked away at a considerable distance. Percival shuffled quickly toward what felt like his purpose. The elevator was far from him now, but he tried not to think about that. He knew he was supposed to stop and go back, but he kept running closer to her. He had no plan B; no other job, no money, no connections, and hardly a family and house, but he tried not to think of that either. His own Pap came to mind; he could be on this floor, too. He wasn't, and Percival had nothing, and with nothing, he charged forward. He felt no less invigorated and more rebellious. A true rebel thinks of nothing to fall back on.

She pushed open the staircase door and was gone. Percival quickly caught up to the door and pushed it open.

"Miss? ... Miss!" He traveled down the steps from Floor 12 to Floor 9 with a hopeful smile. He peered over the railing and saw her on the bottom floor exiting the stairwell. Percival pounced down the steps as fast as his feet could go. Toppling in stumbles and tangled feet, he gripped the handrail. He peered down again and saw her standing still, peering up at him.

"Hello," he said as she pushed through the door before he could finish.

Percival quickly shuffled down the flights of steps, falling with the last set of steps to the bottom, but smiling. Slowly, with a bit more civility, he walked through the door into a hallway he was familiar with. This hall contained the dressing rooms and restrooms for the employees. He had folded own clothes and placed them on a shelf somewhere. She was at some distance down the dark hallway; Percival wasn't sure where until he eyed the cat's tail poking out and then disappearing inside a door. Percival felt a rush of energy that pushed him quickly forward. He reached the door, and the room was dark.

He continued in and switched on the light. The room held shelves of towels and linen that looked familiar, and he thought the locker room was through that room. He walked to the other side of the room when the lights flickered. He looked up briefly, and as he continued, the lights turned off. With only a dimly lit hallway, the room was as black as a black wall pasted to his face. Opening his eyes wider only revealed more of the black wall. Darkness trapped him.

"Hello?" Percival called out. "Can someone turn the—"

A metal shelf rolled in front of him as he turned towards the entrance of the room. It smacked him, causing him to stumble backward. The shelf dominated his space.

"Hello? Are you there?" *I should run*, thought Percival, but he could see nothing. Percival grasped the shelf to guide him to its corner. A second rolling sound split his hearing and shoved against his back. He stumbled toward the other shelf. "I'm not gonna hurt you," Percival managed quietly.

"Then go!" a whisper sounded and chilled Percival's skin. He didn't answer. Petrified, he couldn't answer. The shelf in front of him suddenly rolled away. Percival felt revealed, vulnerable. He couldn't see anything. Could she see him? What would hit him next? He lost direction. Which way was the door?

The other shelf rolled away from him. He couldn't stand there. He felt like a target. Percival started walking forward just to be somewhere else. His forehead hit the corner of another shelf. He sprinted back and started in another direction. Another shelf pushed him, and he was stuck in a corner.

"Please, miss! I just wanna talk to ya," Percival begged with a shaky voice.

Although the lights were still off, Percival could see a shape forming, and he hoped to see her. Instead, the light shaped into a different lady, a maid in uniform. This wasn't the same lady.

"You work for Hugenby, don't you! Hired to get rid of me!" the whisper transformed into a soft voice at the same rate of becoming a veritable person. She stood in front of him with curly hair in a bun, wearing a ruffled apron and a black tea-length, collared dress. She held a folded sheet in her arms.

"No, I don't know you," Percival answered in a monotone voice.

The woman quickly unfolded and spread the sheet into full ripples, snapping it over and over.

"No, but you must leave me alone! Tell Hugenby to leave me alone or else!" The billows of the sheet slapped against Percival. The cat meowed as if giving a warning to one of them. He tried to back up, but a shelf stood behind him. Percival couldn't see her behind the sheet. He panted in frustration and tried to grab the sheet. As the sheet came down, he caught a glimpse of a hat. It was her. The lady!

"Stay away!" she shouted and hissed. His breath relaxed into numbness. He opened his hands. She continued to snap the sheet, and it billowed over Percival's head and covered him. He stood completely still in awe. He breathed the same air she did. If he could have made a tunnel of her breath, he would have slept there. In each breath were her thoughts and the ingredients of her words. He stood still with a sheet over his head.

Finally, after some time of being in awe of the lady's presence, Percival snatched the sheet off his head. There was no one in the room, and the lights were brightly on. Two maids walked into the room.

"Hey, what happened in here?" one of them asked.

Percival grabbed one of the ladies by the shoulders. "Is it you? Please, I won't hurt you! What's your name?" Percival's anguish released onto the maids.

"Get your hands off me, ya' goon! ... Bent on the job, you bum! ... I'll report you to Hugenby, kid!" the ladies shouted at Percival. He backed out of the room and jolted down the hallway. He looked frantically in each opened door but saw no other woman.

I gotta find her! He imagined feeling her arms on either side of him, holding down the sheet. *She was practically hugging me! Under the sheet!* Percival's one focus, uncommon for a Chicagoan. In the city of Chicago which bustled with millions of angles where any living human may place his mind and set it in many places for a while, Percival's one focus was on this woman in the hat with the veil and the pouty lips that spoke to him. He couldn't see her any other way. The rolling shelves showed her playful spirit, he was certain. With searching eyes, he smiled. The beautiful idea of placing him in complete darkness to see nothing but her — who was obviously not darkness — showed her light, her brightness. *She has no darkness in her! She lit up the room! How could such a bright beauty be evil?* A puff of laughter pushed out of his chest and widened his eyes.

He found a section bustling with employees. How would he find her? The chaos in his head kept him from reason: to walk out of the hotel and never come back. More employees scurried back and forth. His boss stood in a doorway.

"Gallivanting, are we, Dooley?" asked Mr. Hugenby with gritted teeth.

9

———————

The Heights of an
Elevator Attendant

Percival followed Mr. Hugenby to the next training session. Mr. Hugenby lashed out at Percival for leaving his elevator.

"She was to come to you!" Mr. Hugenby stopped to look at Percival. He continued and stopped again to say, "In the V. Nolan, your assigned elevator!" He growled as he stomped forward. Percival followed as obsequiously as he could with conflicting loyalty.

"Just one thing, sir. Um, I guess I don't- ... why do you need me to kill her?" Percival spoke to the back of Mr. Hugenby's head.

"You're not killing her because she's not alive!" Mr. Hugenby answered and turned around, facing Percival. "Will that convince you to obey orders?"

The attendants re-assembled on the bottom floor. They all looked at Mr. Hugenby's miserable face and then studied Percival.

"Our expectations are strict and unwavering!" Mr. Hugenby immediately lectured. "Even your outward demeanor, your appearance, your words, your faces. Certain ... poses, I should say, are required."

Percival stationed himself beside Hubert. Claude and Hubert leaned in toward Percival. "What the hell happened to you?" they asked.

"I- I was just ...," Percival quietly chuckled. "I tried to follow a gorgeous woman." He beamed as Hubert and Claude gave "ah"s of approval. Percival looked at Mr. Hugenby, who must have heard him. His face was grave, and his eyes pierced at Percival. Startled, Percival remained focused on the beige walls. Hubert and Claude stared as if waiting to be entertained. Mr. Hugenby stared as if Percival were an enemy.

"We'll start with just your faces," Mr. Hugenby began and pulled his stare away from Percival. "Yes! Your faces, I say! All facial expressions are to be worn as stiff as your uniform and are required to look apathetically professional. Only your few words shall show care, concern. A willingness to sacrifice anything for the guest. A mask, you will find, gives you control of your elevators and gets the job done.

"Now, let me see your apathetic professionalism. Relax the muscles in your face. Keep your mouth closed. Do not narrow your eyes and do not enlarge your eyes. Rest all your face with a slight lift of your eyebrows. On your face, let me see," the man commanded, and he approached Percival first. Percival slightly lifted his eyebrows and rested the rest of his face. It wasn't easy; Percival had natural twitches of eagerness in his sunken face. But he succeeded in appearing quite uncaring, which was precisely how he felt about his ghost-catching mission. If he met his pap, he hoped to express the same lack of care. This was also how he felt about the scathing of Mrs. Wright and Agnes, along with their insults about his drunk mum, about his Irish blood. His work expression armored his face regarding heights.

"Along with your professional face, you must greet all guests before they greet you. You must speak first. We lead and serve; we don't follow and serve." He returned his focus to Percival. Percival pasted on his professional face. Mr. Hugenby stared at him for a moment.

"Well, Dooley, I'm staring right at you! Why don't you greet me?" A laugh murmured quickly and then quieted. Mr. Hugenby continued his test with the other new employees. The other men offered creative greetings:

"Good morning, sir," ...

"Good day, sir," ...

"How excellent to see you, sir," ...

"How can I be of service to you today, sir" (Mr. Hugenby didn't care for the dramatic intonation rolled out with this one, as indicated by a small groan.), ...

"Top of the morning, lad," and with this, Mr. Hugenby replied, "Never say that again."

Mr. Hugenby walked each attendant to his assigned elevator door. Percival was last.

Mr. Hugenby stared at Percival in a way that prompted Percival to expect a growl. Mr. Hugenby strolled toward the elevator. Percival followed. "The V. Nolan, a 1903 Otis elevator, promising charm through the years," Mr. Hugenby droned as he and Percival approached a dark wooden sliding door. The wood was embellished with decorative borders around each of the three rectangular door panels. He used great effort to slide open the door, revealing a half-opened gold gate. He pulled open the gate, shortened one foot from the top. The insides of the elevator posed motionlessly before them. The four walls shined with golden coatings and a black marble handrail around three of the walls, interrupted a few feet by a corner velvet bench.

"It came to us with no roof," continued Mr. Hugenby. "We could see straight up the shaft into tomorrow. So, they wired the ceiling for the chandelier and a mirrored look. Really nice." Percival took his position beside the crank. They turned their heads up to see their faces on the ceiling — a view from above. Percival watched the top of Mr. Hugenby's head carried out of the elevator.

Mr. Hugenby stopped in the hallway and glared at Percival. He transformed from a teacher and boss to something darker. Through his teeth, he sieved out, "Do your job!"

The tension came back. Mr. Hugenby walked out of sight down the hallway, leaving Percival alone at the opened elevator. He shifted his feet and eyes as if left with a child, and he didn't know how to take care of a child.

Percival slid shut the heavy door and then the gate. He was closed in with just a dull lever subdued over to the left side, being still and docile-like. The four walls hovered over him like bodyguards. Why would the lady ever come to him? He sighed and grasped the lever, pulling it with a small jerk. He heard a click and felt lighter as if the elevator was now floating. The lever must have been just between moving and being still, and it moaned with impatience, prompting Percival to continue pulling. The gate sheltered him from the rising elevator doors as the elevator descended.

The elevator now proceeded down in relief as the wooden door slid up out of sight. Then a second wooden door appeared from the floor and disappeared up past the ceiling. Painted calligraphy numbers introduced themselves on each door, as if greeting Percival as his new friends.

"Floor 12, hi ya'... 11, great to see ya'," Percival greeted each new floor as he huffed a laugh. "There ya' are, Floor 10. See ya' later." He took a deep breath, closing his eyelids for escape, and breathed in deeply.

The lever was now pointing in the other direction. Percival pulled it towards him, and it stopped abruptly with a strain. A gallop rolled in his chest, and he handled the lever more gently as Floor 2 crept up. Glass windows adorned the elevator door on Floor 2, and he could see a bellboy and a couple standing and facing him, waiting to come aboard. With more pressure, the elevator stopped; however, it wasn't flush with the floor. He concentrated his eyes and every working sense on handling the lever with precision.

Percival pushed the lever slightly down and finally flush with the floor. The bellboy eyed Percival with silent insults as Percival opened the door. The couple offered proper cordials to Percival without any eye contact. Did they perceive Percival as twenty-years-old? He wasn't sure if they could see the skinny, poor Irish boy that he was. Percival cleared his throat. His temperature rose, and he once again felt the uniform stick to his perspiring body.

"You're an idiot," the bellboy told him as he rolled a cart of suitcases onto the elevator.

"Good evening, madam, ... sir," Percival took great lengths to try his professional face.

"Good evening," they greeted in unison. The couple was Mr. and Mrs. Sam and Anne Sichal. On Floor 16, they were lodging for one week, "a well-deserved getaway." They both asked several questions regarding the accommodations, including, "Will we have 24-hour room service because of Sam here being a light sleeper?" Suddenly Mrs. Sichal began with tiny yet fierce sneezes.

"Strange, you're not catching a cold, are you, dear?" asked her husband.

"No, just a sniffle attack."

They came closer to Floor 16. Percival concentrated with all his strength and focus, and he folded his hand gently around the lever.

"Attack?" her husband repeated.

Percival bent his knees and gave a perfect tug to the lever, stopping flush on Floor 16. He smiled widely.

"Enjoy your stay, Mr. and Mrs. Sichal," he saluted them.

"You're an idiot," repeated the bellboy as he exited the elevator.

Mr. Sichal continued his conversation with Mrs. Sichal as they followed the doorman off the elevator, "But you're only sniffle-attacked by cats."

Percival's smile left him.

Cats?

He slid shut the wooden door and gate and looked around the elevator as if to find something hiding. Recalling the morning's training, Percival stopped on each floor, learning to stop perfectly. He slid open the wooden door on Floor 18, and there stood a man waiting.

The man wore a fedora and a black suit. His skin was darker; probably a Greek or Italian, thought Percival. The first conclusion, however, was that this man couldn't be his pap.

"Good afternoon, sir! Where to?"

"The cigah' room."

The cigar room was on Floor 3, but in the North Wing. Percival remembered this from the training. As the two traveled down, the man took a flask from his jacket, opened it while staring at Percival, and took a swig. At Floor 3, the man stepped into the hallway and asked Percival, "Which way?"

"Yes, sir, methinks ..." Percival scratched his head and peered down the hallway. "It's in the North Wing. The North Wing, ya' see. I can take you, I know me way there—"

"You think I'm gonna be seen with an Irish boy holding my hand to the cigah' room? I'll blow ya' head off and leave ya' body in this fancy elevator before I let you walk me anywhere. Just point, for Christ's sake." Percival pointed to the right, and the man walked away. Percival's cheeks stung as if he'd been slapped in the face. His face twitched. He forgot how to display apathy. He held the lever, and he and the elevator descended to Floor 2.

No one was waiting at Floor 2, so he stepped off the elevator and waited. Guests strolled by, dressed for dining and nightlife. Percival glared at the guests, combing through the faces. Where was his pap? And where was Charlie?

"Hey!" a voice scratched beside him. It was Hubert Downey. "What happened to you? We thought you got canned. Is this your elevator today?"

"Yeah, and this one's yours?" Percival exchanged.

"Oh yeah. Busy day. My feet are done, you know?"

Two ladies approached Hubert's elevator. He greeted them, and they giggled as they boarded his elevator.

"See ya' later, my friend," Hubert said smiling as his door slid shut.

Mr. Hugenby came soon after and approached Percival. Percival had forgotten about the lady and his for the moment, but not Charlie.

"Go home. Be here at five in the morning. You'd best be more effective tomorrow."

Percival felt no apprehension regarding tomorrow; after all, how could tomorrow possibly be as absurd as today? Well, there was a cat.

10

Rex Dooley

Rex Dooley gaped at the butter frosted in dollops on his thickly sliced bread. His lips swelled with the aroma of the speckled honey, and he tried to keep his eyes layered upon it as he sank his teeth into a large bite of the soft, warm bread. With his eyes rolled upward and closed, he grunted with "Mmm, oh yeah," filtered through the bread stuffed full in his mouth, his eyes still closed. He swallowed the bread and licked his lips with his eyes still closed, and finally opened them to see the crowd staring at him with no expression. He stared back for a moment, inconspicuously loving the taste in his mouth.

Rex stood center stage and held out his arms to each side, swallowed again, and exclaimed in his low voice, "That was good hot bread, ladies and gentlemen!" He swayed left to right. The crowd snickered in scattered spots. "Get your own hot bread tonight in Trouer Tower just upstairs above our heads." He pointed up and looked at the ceiling as if he could see the excitement on the second floor.

Rex was friends with the owner's son, Wyatt Trouer. The Trouers called their upstairs restaurant "The Trouer Tower." Downstairs had no name; Mr. Trouer was careful to keep his fully stocked refuge a secret from police. Only those with a passcode could enter.

"May I speak to the owner, please?" a dining guest would say.

Upon arriving at the table, the guest who wasn't part of his inner circle would give Mr. Trouer the passcode:

"Should we leave the candle on the table burning or blow it out?"

Mr. Trouer would respond by placing a small invitation on the table, dated for one-night-only entry. After eating their dinner, the guests retreated down a hallway beside the kitchen to a dirty, gray metal door. They'd give their invitation to a man nearby, who'd open the door for them, revealing spiral steps in a dimly lit stairwell. Access to the speakeasy had no blatant marks. Wyatt helped his father run the business.

Wyatt previously joined Rex in opening the bird-tagging business. When Free on a Leash failed and they were both out of work, Mr. Trouer allowed Rex to host the speakeasy from time to time. Unlike his brother, Rex craved heights. He instinctively dreamed of how to get up there.

The back of the Trouer building was for trash and for employees to enter and exit. The alley was dark, and it's where Percival found a barrel to lean against and wait for his brother to exit. Rex exited as he always did, busting open the door and laughing, looking around as if he'd never been outside before. His mustache was getting shabby, yet somehow his smile was still obvious.

"Me jar! Me mucker!" Rex slurred on seeing Percival. "What is this get-up? This blue dance suit?" They walked together down the dark road toward home. Rex danced along the way.

"Tis no dance suit, Rex," Percival answered. He always thickened his Irish accent around his brother, for no known reason why. "I'm wearing me uniform."

Rex drew his head closer to see "*BH*" embroidered on Percival's lapel. "The Blaughvoyon Hotel?"

"I'm the elevator attendant — well, one of 'em."

"Yes! Your new work, and ..." Rex started and then studied Percival's face as they walked. "You work in the air? With heights?"

Percival shrugged his shoulders in frustration and shook his head.

"Are ya' scared?"

"Rex, lemme ask you, why don't they place soft landings at the bottom of elevators?"

"Cause they don't land."

"An elevator crashed in the hotel today," Percival refuted, and the gravity of his emotions resurfaced. "Crashed to the bottom! Just this day!"

"Were you in it?" asked Rex. A plausible question, and as they pondered the elevation issue, they agreed on two things: Percival would fall again, and Percival's luck with life had to have been running out. So, something had to be done.

"We could switch jobs," suggested Rex.

"Work in a bar? I already asked Mr. Trouer, Rex." Of course, Percival had no intentions of leaving his job. He pushed aside his first thought of his pap and replaced it with the thought of the lady in the hat; he didn't want to leave the Blaughvoyon Hotel. He wanted to see her and protect her. His day was too much to unload on his brother all at once, so he didn't yet mention the lady nor Pap. Also, Rex's determination to rid Percival of fear developed into his new mission.

Finally, questions unfolded a plan. The brothers turned around. They walked back toward the hotel. Rex wore a winning smile as he walked, and Percival found comfort in his brother's competence. Percival knew Rex's ideas and actions were consistently absurd and dangerous, and an uncanny number of friends agreed with Rex's innovations. Percival was his most agreeable fan. Rex had never been injured, although Rex's actions pointed him straight to broken bones, bullets, and breathlessness. He had plenty of nasty outcomes, but he didn't die. Such was the Dooley standard of a successful day — don't die.

Percival entered the back employee door as Rex entered the front of the hotel. Percival wasn't convinced the hotel security would let Rex in. But there in the lobby lounged Rex, speaking with a couple who frequented the Trouer Tower.

Percival thought now could've been a suitable moment for Pap to be discovered.

"Alright, Percy," Rex swayed with his knees slightly bent and feet apart. "Lead the way." Percival motioned for Rex to follow him down to Floor 1. The day was ending, and the hallway at the bottom of the hotel was dark. Their shuffling feet were the only sounds in the long hallway. Dark shadows cast past corners and doorways. Some seemed to move a bit. Open doors with dark spaces chilled Percival's nerves.

"Here, I think, is my elevator," whispered Percival. He opened a door to an empty, dark pit with an Otis engine. Rex stepped down into the pit and looked up. The elevator rested just one floor up.

Percival felt a coldness behind him and wished Rex wouldn't stand inside the pit. Was a ghost nearby? He looked down the dark hallway.

"Percy?" Rex suddenly stood in front of Percival and caused Percival to gasp. Together, they walked the L-shape of the hallway from the elevator pit to the bedding supply room. Hotel employees passed Rex and Percival a few times, but none of them questioned the brothers. As they filled their arms with pillows, they agreed the task was ridiculous. They also agreed that Percival would fall down the elevator shaft in some unknown, unpredictable way. It would happen, and considering this knowledge was fact, they had to plan ahead and give Percival some peace when he was high in the air. Pillows helped with the fall of an elevator as much as a hand covering a head helped amid a tornado. These things assure; they don't save.

Two trips conjured a fluffy pile in the elevator pit. Rex and Percival stood and stared at their work. Percival admitted to dropping a potato cake down the shaft, sharing a laugh. Rex reached inside his coat and pulled out some wrapped potato cakes. He threw them on top of the pillows.

"Some extra fluff," he mumbled. They weren't fluffy nor less than two days old.

Percival was eager to get outside, away from the eerie darkness of the hotel's bottom floor, away from what he couldn't see.

"What are you thinking about? Your smile is scaring me," Rex commented and stared at Percival as they walked under the streetlights.

Percival chuckled. "I'm thinking about a woman," he answered with a full-teeth smile. "I met the most beautiful gal in the hotel, Rex. She looks like a painting. And turns out she was probably not even a real girl ... just my imagination."

"Your mind is crazier than mine, I tell ya'."

"But I'm gonna find her anyway, ya' know? I gotta."

"Who? The lady in your dreams?" Rex gave his hips a swing with his words.

"Yes."

"Good. Don't give up." They walked in silence for a while.

"Rex, do you believe in ghosts?"

"Yes, absolutely," Rex quickly answered. "One lives in the speakeasy. Some old Revolutionary War soldier who wants a drink."

"You've seen him?"

"Maybe. A man in this filthy, raggedy old costume—looked like he just came off the battlefield—he approached me one day, and he said to me, 'Gimme a drink, ya' damn Irishman!'" Rex shouted. Percival turned his head to see his surroundings. Rex spread his hands out as if preparing to give a soliloquy. "So, I poured him a scotch, and I turned around, and he was gone. He disappeared! Poof!"

The brothers walked in silence for another moment, and Rex lowered his voice, "Trouer says he walks around the bar like he's looking for a way out, looking out the windows. But he won't go through the door and leave. Heh, heh."

"You mean like he's stuck there?"

"Well, now that you mention it, yeah, maybe so," Rex contemplated. "Do you believe in ghosts, Percy? Did you see a ghost at the hotel today? ... Ah! You did! The gal? Or 'the painting,' like you said."

"Maybe."

"And how did she like your blue dance suit?"

Percival smiled. Perhaps the painting did like his uniform. Perhaps he loved her. It might not add up to be love at all, but love opened the door, Percival was certain. Bliss is nice to bask in until reality dissipates it.

Such was the case at 4:00 in the morning in their South Side Chicago home. Poof.

11

Lena Dooley

A killer on the loose! A killer, me say!" Mrs. Lena Dooley screamed throughout their small, two-room house at four in the morning. Percival and Rex rose after having lain down an hour before. Lena had just gotten home from her barmaid job at a small, incognito pub attached to the nearby metal factory. Neighbors picked Mr. Wright up and took him into the Wright house. They laid his body on the bed.

"I come home from me bar duties and see him lying right there on the ground! Something just didn't look right! Me knows plastered when me sees it, and me knows dead when me sees it. Mr. Wright- he was murdered indeed!"

"Murdered, Mum?" questioned Percival.

"Mum, why ..." Rex began.

"I don't know why, Rex. Why would anyone partake in such a heinous crime! He was already a drunkard, bound to go soon with no help!" When their mother came home in the deep hours of the night from work, Mr. Wright's face was swollen and blue. They stood and watched as Lena sat with Mrs. Wright and hugged her as they both cried.

Lena may have been crying for herself. As a growing girl in Ireland, Lena's father, Patty Carroll, raised her. As a stout girl with a loud voice, a bit rough around her husky edges, she often accompanied her father's local Irish pub as the bar helper, where she laughed with her mouth open, swore, danced, and sang as loud as any of them. Her assertive roughness was polished with more roughness, if there could have been such a thing. The town of frail Irish women who stayed home and kept quiet frowned upon Lena's stomping and shouting and drinking and laughing. It mattered none to her, for she had caught the eye of a tall, slim man of books and poetry — Mathew Dooley. She was different in his eyes- a good different, something he searched for in his books but could never find, and he fell in love with Lena. He often visited the pub to see her. He tried to keep his dislike for alcohol a secret. Mr. Carroll helped by serving Mathew tea. Lena smiled with a more fulfilled joy when he came into the pub. They both beamed. She was in love. Mr. Carroll knew his beloved daughter found her destiny. Despite the heckles of disapproval, the couple wedded in the bar, around the regulars who witnessed the blooming of the Dooley love.

The couple both had an echo comprised in the middle of their throats, as if there was a tunnel somewhere in there. And this was another thing Mathew Dooley loved about Lena. The first sound they both expressed within each other's hearing range resounded as if one of them was going to sing.

Their lowly Irish voices spoke a pleasing baritone lull, as an Irish low whistle. Lena's and Mathew's voices were more confident than any warrior Ireland had ever heard or wanted to hear. After Lena's father died, she and her new husband left to find acceptance and money from a new magical part of the world, Chicago.

Now, in Chicago's South Side, neighbors slowly left the Wright house and bid condolences to the weeping Mrs. Wright. Lena sat with Mrs. Wright and cried and held her close. Rex picked up a liquor bottle and examined it.

"He spits in it," Agnes warned. Rex and Percival made their way out, seeing how Agnes expressed no need for a visit. Lena and Mrs. Wright sat still on the bed and sniffed and wailed. Amidst these mourning ladies, Mr. Wright sat up.

"Where's my fags, you dreadful whore?" he slurred and gargled out.

Mrs. Wright turned white and flustered with an open mouth; then she shouted, "It's a miracle! Thank Heavens!"

Lena snapped her head from the Mr. to the Mrs., wiped her face dry with her chubby hands, and she exploded into a mess of frustration. With a growl, Lena charged after Mr. Wright. She grabbed his hair in one hand and his collar in the other, and slammed him against the frame of the door. "He's no miracle. He's a demon raised from the dead. He's a demon!" Lena shouted in Mr. Wright's face. "Back out in the mud ya' go!" Mrs. Wright gave high-pitched protests behind Lena's thunderous voice. Rex and Percival reappeared at the door and moved quickly as Lena threw Mr. Wright in the mud by his home. "Ye no good! A wicked man!"

"Hah!" shouted Mr. Wright. "You're a poor wife! A terrible wife! Ha! Ha! So bad, he left you, didn't he? Left you alone! Ha! Ha! All alone, the large and bad wife Dooley! All alone!"

"Shuttup, dead man!" Rex shouted.

Lena stood back and breathed hard. She walked with her sons back to their own home next-door, just three feet away. Rex turned to give Mr. Wright a kick with a bird call. As he entered his home, Percival came out and gave Mr. Wright two more kicks and walked back into his home. As Percival closed the door, Agnes came out of her house, stood over Mr. Wright, and dropped a cigarette in his lap. She hesitated before walking back into the house, turned around, and gave Mr. Wright a soft kick before going back inside.

Mrs. Dooley moaned and talked to herself as she cooked morning potato cakes.

"Poor, poor woman... If only me own Dooley would come through the door... He left me. He left me for good..."

"You're a good wife and a good Mum," comforted her sons. "We'll find him."

"Maybe soon, Mum! Maybe, ya' know, maybe he's right here in Chicago," Percival tried.

"Chicago?" Lena questioned. "He's not in Chicago." The Wrights may have been right; if Mathew Dooley was still alive, they'd only find a bad man. Percival didn't want to see Pap, but he and Rex knew their mother needed closure.

"Me Mathew. Oh, me Mathew. Where'd ya' go? Why'd ya' leave me? Why'd ye leave your wife, huh?"

At each day's end, she often shared with many, "He'll be by me side when me awakes." The next morning, after morning, after morning, she opened her eyes to his empty fluffy pillow.

"He'll be home to lie by me before the day ends," she used to say. Percival and Rex bade her goodnight and goodnight and goodnight as she walked to the dark corner to her bed alone.

The upcoming trip to Ireland lifted her sadness. She packed something daily.

"Where, Mum, do you think Pap is?" asked Rex in his years of youth.

"He's lost, me Rex. And then he finds his way but gets stuck, Rex," Lena answered with her eyes fixed as if she could see him. She stood to fill her tin cup. "But ya know what happens next? He gets unstuck, and he gets lost. Again." It was all a guess, of course. Guessing was all she could do in blindness and memories. Back in Ireland, a younger Mathew read *The Odyssey* to the younger Lena. She became exhausted with the book — "bad luck after bad luck."

Mathew quickly shared the ending with her, "He made it home to his beloved Penelope, Lena. Love is stronger than bad luck, Lena." He promised he'd be home quickly.

"If I not," Mathew answered, "hope me dead, me Lena. Hope me dead."

"Never, me love," she answered.

Mathew protested, "Why would ya' hope me still living? I would be with you if I was living. Ah, it breaks me, love. I'd never stay away from you, me love. Don't ya' know I love ya'? I'll always love ya', Lena. You're the pulse of me heart. Me *Acushla.* If you hope me to be alive and leave you alone, then you hope I don't love ya'. Hope me dead, Lena."

Percival had heaviness in his chest for knowing something. He wanted to speak. He'd find Charlie the next morning at work.

12

Percival Dooley

Percival would never hurt the lady they called a ghost, and when he found his pap, he planned to punch him hard in the face. His mum shouldn't have had to suffer so. No lady should, except Agnes and Mrs. Wright.

Every morning, Percival didn't lie on his back because it made him look dead. His rib cage flared up high as his stomach caved low. He awoke thinking of so much, but for the sake of sanity, he focused on the beautiful lady. A desire to save her gave him a pull out of bed. He moved quietly to wake no one. In the lavatory, with a burst of his face and neck scrubbing, a man in an apron appeared behind him holding a sack. Percival quickly turned around.

"Percival Dooley, right?" the man asked. Percival nodded. "The boss said you'd be up. Here, take it to your family and get to work." The man shoved the sack into Percival's chest and looked around. "You don't live in here, do you?"

"No," Percival answered. He dried his face with his arm and returned to his house with the sack. Before opening the door, he saw Mrs. Wright awake and up. She agreed to give the sack of food to Lena.

As Percival walked to work, a chill bit at his face. A gust of wind tunneled through the houses and pushed him. Winter didn't want to leave quietly. Pap wasn't around last night to defend Percival's mother.

"Stay outta me way, Pap! I'm gonna punch ya'! I'll punch ya' right in the face, Pap!" Percival breathed out, noticing his lips forming his thoughts, and he huffed out a laugh. The dark sky pushed down the sun, and Lena's grief from last night bothered Percival still. The maze of homes blackened his path. Occasional beams whispered out from a few windows and relieved Percival's steps from puddles, mud, and trash. Scattered scuffles of mumbling and distant conversations with the occasional wail from a child comforted Percival of the truth that life went on. He walked forward to find Charlie.

Past the neighborhood across a black paved street took him to bigger buildings. The tops of the buildings again spat out its smokes to the gray air. He'd find the beautiful woman. Percival pushed each step with hands in his pockets. He wasn't doing Mr. Blaughvoyon's side work of slaying her.

Kill a woman? She was tricky, an enigma. Could she be …

"Who are you?" Percival asked the air. "Why are you at the hotel? Why don't you just leave?" He slowed his steps. Percival's thoughts confused him. He strolled forward to the massive hotel that reached high. Despite his issue with air, he'd find his pap.

He stopped and looked behind him at the familiarity, and then ahead. Level ground was comforting. He had never conquered heights and never descended gracefully. It had nothing to do with fear. It wasn't a fear of heights; it was the logic of heights. What wasn't logical was to hang in the air and try to slay an inconspicuous ghost. He resumed the walk. More pedestrians came and went around him, and he liked their company.

As the hotel came into sight, too much was in his head. His face twitched. Percival saw its windows turn into eyes and stare at Percival. Some eyes were lit, some were dark and hiding. Some changed their inside shapes and silhouettes, like the small thoughts moving around behind the eyes, looking at him. He tried not to gasp as twitches danced around his wide eyes. The gray sky was turning midnight blue. The smoke continued to dance. He earned the right to at least be more hesitant than most. He still tried to be as intrepid as Rex.

There were presently no heights; and so he stood in humiliation and stared down at the mottled pavement as people hurried by.

He breathed in, looked both ways, and shook his head as if to confirm some bad idea. Percival inhaled deeply and walked toward the hotel. He looked up again and saw the windows where they belonged. He peered closer, and he longed to see his lady. An added skip and bounce directed him to the employee entrance and the check-in quarters. Percival looked around, wondering if the walls were breathing or moving.

"Dooley, go wash your face. You look like hell. Try to appear put together, for crying out loud," commanded William Walden, a hospitality lead. "Then, you got the same elevator as yesterday. The V. Nolan." In the employee locker room were other attendants reprimanded for dusty shoes, spots on jackets, smells, and untamed hair.

Percival's elevator was open at Floor 2, waiting for him. He had things to do, but he took his post, stood firm, and thought of the lady, his pap, Charlie, and the pillows under his feet.

13

The V. Nolan Elevator

The early morning lobby, still sparse of customers, was richly shiny. The whirl of the staircase banister, the billowy shine of the black floor, the golden gilt around the service desk, and like a wallflower, Percival's own elevator. He was a part of it at the moment as a prop. Percival preferred this role over being elevated 30 floors or more in the air. He preferred it over being a bounty hunter after a ghost. Yet, dutifully, he eyed each woman passing; *could she be ... her?* Each man passing; *Pap?*

He straightened up and felt pleasantly surprised when Charlie walked toward him carrying a brown bag.

"Get in. Get in," Charlie ordered as he walked into the elevator with Percival. "Here." Charlie handed the bag to Percival and slid shut the door and the gate. Percival didn't remember him as so tall and broad. He looked at Percival in surprise.

"Are you kidding me?" Charlie spoke lowly as if someone was listening. "You don't even know food when you see it, you pathetic bagga' bones," Percival helped himself to the roll, sausage, and a bottle of cider in the bag. He managed a "thank you" with a full mouth.

"The sack of food to your house, you got it, correct?" asked Charlie. Percival nodded his head and kept chewing.

"Slow down. Don't make ya'self sick, son."

Percival stopped chewing. "What?"

Charlie swept away the pause quickly. "Don't look at me; I'm no pop, Dooley, but I can't let you work here looking so pathetic. Fill your stomach. You get hungry, you come find me — and I'm no pop."

"Where's me Pap?" Percival asked. "He's here somewhere. I wanna see him and get it over with."

"What are you talking about?" Charlie asked. "Who told you your father was here?"

"Y- Didn't you?"

"No, kid. What, you were lookin' for him? That's really pathetic. Cause you don't listen, do you?" Charlie took the paper bag and slid open the gate. Before he slid open the gate and left, he concluded, "Things are gonna unfold for ya' soon. Just do your job and trust me."

"Yeah, but it's a whole lot more than-"

"Stop right there," Charlie spoke with his hand up as he walked away. "Pathetic *and* lazy is not a good look."

Percival didn't have time to think about Charlie's words. Three shiny-faced men in overcoats stumbled toward Percival.

Charlie greeted them as he kept walking, "Safe travels home, gentlemen."

Their shirts had lost their crisp. Two of them gripped the arms of a much younger man between them. The younger man had a bloody lip and a dark, swollen eye. Thoughts of ghost-finding and Pap-punching left Percival. The men scurried into the elevator. The youngest slumped on the corner bench inside. Stout liquor odors and cigar smoke permeated the air. Percival stared at the men.

"What are you doing? Fifth floor!" the oldest man snapped at Percival.

Percival answered, "Oh, right, yes, sir." He closed the door and gate with a huff of a laugh, and he refreshed his memory as he gripped the crank. He also concluded none must be his pap. But was his pap even here at the hotel?

"Wait a minute, Mr. Elevator Boy," said the bloody-lipped young man with a chuckle. "Where are we going?" He motioned for Percival to be still with the crank. The other two men shouted with grunts and spit and clinched teeth.

"The fifth floor, as requested," answered Percival.

"Go! Keep going!" shouted the oldest gentleman.

"Every time we go out, Ren!" and "You're gonna get us shot!" and "You're apologizing and we're going home!" The younger gentleman — "Ren" — slicked back his hair and pressed it down with his fedora. Percival felt calm as well, despite the havoc. Their monstrosities were theirs, not Percival's.

A light shone on the third floor. "Third floor for a pickup, sirs," Percival announced as he stopped the elevator and opened the door.

A woman in a short green shimmy dress stood waiting to get on. She wasn't wearing typical early morning attire. A beautiful woman, too beautiful to be real. She rushed in as the door opened and faced the younger man, Ren.

"You poor man," she soothingly flirted. She glanced over at Percival and then down.

"Madam," Percival greeted as he stared at her. *A woman, all alone and beautiful - she must be unreal!*

"I'm okay, doll," Ren answered. "I'm okay. But ask Elevator Boy. How's he doing? He looks like somethin's on his mind." With this, the woman gazed at Percival with a soft smile and silence.

"What? I mean, sir, no, me- I got nothing on me mind," Percival mumbled out. He glanced over at the lady. "Your name? What's your name, madam?" Percival's voice quivered out. Ren heckled lightly in the background.

The woman stared at Percival and answered, "Why do you want my name?" If fluid poured slowly, like royalty walking, it would be her voice.

"Have we met before?" Percival asked; he gulped before adding, "And the cat?"

"I think the question you want to ask me — what I'm typically asked in this situation, is 'What floor.' My name nor our previous encounters, nor... a cat? has anything to do with the two of us going up or down, now does it?"

Percival basked in her beauty. *It's her!* He knew it.

"Fifteenth floor, by the way," she added.

"Do ya' mean the fourteenth floor?"

"No, why would I make that mistake?"

"Aren't ya' staying on the fourteenth?"

"Fifteenth."

"But you have to remember. We met on Floor 14. You had your luggage and your cat."

"Really?" the woman inquired. "Am I truly mistaken? But I don't remember meeting you." She took a key out of her purse. "Yes, see here. Floor 15. Besides, I don't have a cat. I've seen a old cat roaming around, but it's not mine. Those things are dreadful!"

She looked at Ren again with a smile and said, "Listen to me. I have a room on the fifteenth floor. You can come get cleaned up and get something to eat brought up to the room."

"No," answered the older man, "we're going to the cigar room and home. We're not staying in Chicago."

"We can go up for a minute first, old man," said Ren. "Hey, fella, the fifteenth floor. Then you and I'll find the cat broad on the fourteenth floor. How's that sound?" He said with a wink. Percival banged shut the door and gate and reached for his lever before he stood beside it. He didn't hear the disagreement in the background.

How would he know if this woman was his lady in disguise?

Silly thought — She's a woman, not a ghost.

But what if? What if she's the ghost in disguise? What if she needs his help? Or, what if she plans to kill all the men on the elevator? What if a sixteen-year-old boy just wants to talk to the pretty lady? Doesn't any excuse suffice?

Mr. Blaughvoyon and Mr. Hugenby gave Percival instructions — Percival remembered — on how to catch a ghost, how to tell if a passenger was a ghost, and how to suffocate a ghost. All he had to do was stop the elevator, and she would respond, giving him his answer. He didn't exactly want to catch her. He didn't want to catch anyone nor anything. But what if she was the beautiful lady in disguise? How could he help her unless he was sure?

What if he stopped the elevator just to see what happened? If she felt suffocated, then he'd know. He wouldn't try to hurt her. He definitely wouldn't let her die; he just wanted to know. But if he stopped the elevator with the men inside, would Percival survive the stop? They'd probably pound him to a pulp. It was too complicated to try. Too many risks were involved. But if he didn't try, ...

He placed his hand on the lever and stared at his hand. The elevator continued up. He couldn't pull it. He saw the fourth floor fly down. Before it slipped away, Percival closed his eyes and pulled the elevator to a halt. They were in-between floors. He stared ahead for a moment, thankful no one was yet more contentious than he attempted to portray himself. The elevator creaked. Percival turned and stared at the lady.

"What the hell are you doing!" the older man shouted. Percival continued to stare at the lady. She looked back at him with the corner of her eye.

"What's wrong with this guy?" Ren asked as he stayed sitting. "Crazy night! Do you two know each other?"

"I beg your pardon, young man," asked the lady, "but do we know each other?"

"Do we?" Percival strained out.

"You obviously seem to think so."

"I'm not moving the elevator. What do ya' think about that?" Everyone stood still. The woman looked at the three gentlemen behind and around her and back at Percival. Percival didn't hide his need for a deep breath.

"Ren, no!" shouted the other man. Percival looked over to see Ren's hand cupped as it pinned him to the wall.

"I can handle this," the lady told the men. With her hand on Ren's shoulder, he let go. She gave her attention to Percival. She had to be the ghost. They stood and faced one another, and she walked closer to him.

"How old are you?" she asked.

"I'm twenty years old."

The men laughed.

"Yes. I do remember you. Bailey Park, earlier this year. If you're truly twenty."

Percival stood frozen for a noticeable moment. "What? ... No, I — ya' got me mistaken." Percival smoothed out. "I'm sorry." She was still as beautiful and as calm as she was outside the elevator. She wasn't suffering from the entrapment, except for his stare and forced imprisonment.

"But, one question," the lady began, "who do you think I am?"

"I'm so sorry," he blurted. He pulled the lever to go to the fifteenth floor with a resting smile toward the falling wall of numbers.

"What happened in Bailey Park?" Ren asked.

"We were at the top of the world in the deep South, and he broke my heart," the lady answered as she gazed at Percival.

"No. I've never been down to the south part of- of the ... of the country," answered Percival, still smiling.

The door of the fifteenth floor flew down into view. The lady was first to exit with a soft "bye." Each of the three men gave Percival a pat on the shoulder. Ren was the last to get off.

"Don't worry, amigo," he whispered. "I don't know her name either!"

Who was she? Perhaps Percival should have waited longer to see the effects. But would he have? Would he be able to watch the woman of his dreams suffer from suffocation?

Before pushing the lever to Floor 2, Percival slouched in the corner bench with a winning smile, the kind of smile everyone works and toils and sweats for, even more than money. He felt his potato cake in his jacket pocket.

"Well, Mr. Potato Cake, can ya' dive fast like an elevator?" Percival pulled the lever, and the elevator jerked with a short fall, as in four centimeters of a fall. This wiped off Percival's smile and pushed out a small chuckle. He peered through the crack, and with a deep breath, he dropped the cake through. His breath became deeper as he looked away and breathed out another small laugh.

On to his next mission: Find the ghost lady. On his way down, he wondered what her name might be:

Dove,

Lily,

maybe Rose,

Dorothy, or even Sunshine. He slouched in the corner bench as he descended.

Down to Floor 2 stood Mr. and Mrs. Mercier, glaring at him. Percival jolted up almost at attention. The couple boarded with a stare one would use when blackmailing someone, to intimidate someone, to dare someone. In her brown fur coat, Mrs. Mercier held her cigarette in a long black holder adorned with gems.

She pranced onto the elevator and said, "To zee stockholder's meeting, s'il vous plaît."

Percival did not know the meeting's whereabouts. He closed the door and gate, and he placed his hand on the lever and pulled. The elevator jerked and rose as slowly as warm air. Mrs. Mercier puffed her cigarette. Percival turned to see both staring at him. He smiled and faced the front.

"Something fell," Mrs. Mercier said.

"I beg your pardon?"

"Something fell. I saw it. It fell from the elevator. What was it?"

"I," Percival shrugged, "I can't say."

The door's floor numbers appeared and fell beneath the floor.

Floor 8, …

Floor 9, …

Floor 10, … he continued and tried to think. *Did we talk about this meeting floor in the training?*

She interrupted his ignorance: "You're Irish, no?"

"Yes, madam."

"How did you get the job? You know someone. Have connections?" she probed.

"Have you met our son, Claude?" Mr. Mercier chimed in.

"Oh, yes, yes. I have. Um,"—

"Claude is incredibly talented and works here to help Nick."

"You know," Mrs. Mercier said, "Monsieur Blaughvoyon," she added with a trill. "You met him?"

"What? Oh, yes," answered Percival. Mrs. Mercier laughed.

"I thought he was"—started Mr. Mercier.

"Shut up, dear," his wife answered.

The ride to nowhere was long. Floor 14, … Floor 15…

"Where *are* you taking us?" Mrs. Mercier asked.

"Oh, I'm sorry," Percival said and stopped the elevator. "I will just reverse the elevator." He began back down, and he bade the elevator to just go and not ask questions. "Floor 15."

"It's not zee 15th floor," Mrs. Mercier said.

"Then 14, madam?"

"No! Further up, attendant!" With this, Percival stopped the elevator and started up again. "Floor 31. You did not know? Is it not your job? I suppose you should ask Claude if you have questions," she gave a trill again. "You seem to have some learning to do."

Each number on each door looked in to see the tension and fell down timidly, falling to get away.

Floor 17 ...

Floor 18 ...

"Your name, attendant?" asked Mr. Mercier.

"Dooley, sir. Percival Dooley." Percival felt a burning spot in the back of his head from their eyes.

"Dooley, ... of course," Mrs. Mercier blew her smoke resonantly as if she endowed breezes to the earth's atmosphere.

Floor 22 should have passed by a while ago. If Mrs. Mercier was the ghost in disguise, he'd have had to take his chances and let her go. And Percival hoped Mrs. Mercier wasn't; he'd fall out of admiration quickly. He was the one feeling suffocated. Seeing the 31 on the door softened Percival's mood, but she stood in the elevator for too long a moment as the door waited open for her. He tightened his face again.

Following her husband off the elevator, Mrs. Mercier paused and said, "I have a suite on zee 12th floor, so, Dooley, I will be watching you, and you may call me Dawn." She pranced quickly down the hall. He watched the prominent couple walk away as they floated in the air with no wings.

Percival had a long way to go down from Floor 31. He pictured the height and the air in between him and the surface of the river — *no, not a river. The bottom floor,* he thought and breathed out a laugh. It was a shorter laugh than usual; the Merciers left a dullness in the elevator. A light shone, and he stopped at Floor 22.

A man with thinning hair on a powerful head and dusty work clothes stared at Percival curiously as he walked in.

"Good morning, sir. Where to?" asked Percival as calmly as he could pull off.

"Floor 30. You new here? I've never seen you," the man piped loudly.

Percival snapped back quickly, "Yes sir, yeah, I'm new. I've been here more than a week now." He was still breathing out relief from releasing the Merciers. He realized the passenger detected his aggravation. "I'm sorry; I just"-

"You don't owe me an answer of no kind. People always wantin' to know your business. You don't owe me nothing."

"Thank you, sir," Percival said. He kept his hand on the lever.

"Myself, I've always lived by the notion — I don't owe nobody an explanation for nothing. Good stuff. The bad. I don't tell nobody. I don't intend to," the man said. "You get the here and now. That's it. Ya' know? If it's not good enough, not my problem. Stop bothering me, right? ... I don't owe you nothing... I've always lived by that rule."

His rules seemed congruous with the ghost lady's mannerisms. She never gave Percival an explanation, as if she felt she didn't need to. Surely she hadn't appeared as this grim man, had she? But how ingenious that would be, stopping and trapping a brute man in the elevator was a frightening act. Perhaps she tried to explain how she felt through this intimidating, manly shell.

Percival nodded as he placed his hand on the lever. He wouldn't hurt her, just see if this man was the lady. How much he wanted to escape the elevator, not trap himself with a burly stranger who may be an evil ghost! The elevator continued climbing. Without thinking, he stopped it. For a moment, all was still.

"Why are we stopped?" the man asked.

"I- I need a minute," Percival answered with his back to the man.

"A minute for what? Start the elevator."

"Yes, but I beg you. Give me a minute."

"No, I gotta get to work," his loud voice escalated more. "Start it. NOW!"

"Are you okay, sir?"-

The man lunged towards Percival, grabbed his lapel, and pinned Percival to the wall. "No, I'm not okay!" he shouted through gritted teeth in Percival's face. This was it. He hoped her true identity would be revealed soon. The man felt imprisoned, and he was undoubtedly suffocating.

He then let go of Percival, shook his head, and sat down. "I'm okay. It's okay. Take your time. Don't get all balled up!" said the man. He and Percival remained quiet for a moment.

Nothing changed. The man was fine being imprisoned on the elevator. He sat still and slouched, staring at the floor, thinking of something that was clearly none of Percival's business. This was just a human. A man tired of making excuses and tired of fighting through walls. Percival pulled the lever onward to Floor 30. The man departed without a word.

Percival began the elevator back down, suddenly feeling squeezed in himself. He stopped the elevator on Floor 29 and scurried down hallways for a few moments, looking for the lady. Returning to the V. Nolan, he dropped to Floor 28, got out, and searched for her again. On each floor, he looked for her, skipping Floor 24 at Mr. Blaughvoyon's penthouse. He was grateful for the stability of the flooring in each hallway.

At Floor 23, Percival opened the gate and then the door. Mr. Blaughvoyon suddenly appeared at the door's opening. He blocked Percival's path into the hallway. With his black sunglasses in the middle of his long face, he stared down at Percival.

"What is wrong with you!" scratched Mr. Blaughvoyon's voice. "Are my commands not clear?" The twirls of his mustache slightly trembled, and he gritted his teeth.

"Sir, I ..." Percival had nothing appeasing to say.

Mr. Blaughvoyon stared at Percival. "What are you meddling in, Dooley? Trying things your own way, eh?" Mr. Blaughvoyon heckled with a thin smile. "You won't get anything past me. Finish your assignment immediately!" With that, Mr. Blaughvoyon fled down the hall so quickly he almost looked as if he levitated. Percival remained frozen for a long moment before closing the elevator door and gate.

As he approached Floor 15, he remembered the girl he met earlier, but he didn't want to see her again. Relieved to see no one, he dropped to Floor 14.

He exited the elevator and turned right, seeing a lady's glove on the floor. Percival's heart and feet skipped, and he quickly picked up the glove. At the corner of the hallway, the calico cat's tail waved at him and disappeared. Percival smiled and scurried to take the corner turn. He bumped into a couple holding hands coming the other way. They expressed their "oh my's" and "excuse me's" as they walled Percival from going any further for a noticeable moment. Behind them, further down the hallway, he saw the old cat. It moved slowly but as quickly as it was able. From another corner, the woman, as beautiful as a painting, appeared and noticed Percival. Percival froze in fear. She turned back to walk away.

"Sir, can you take us to the famous V. Nolan elevator?" asked the couple, stopped and facing him. "Sir?"

"Yes, that's my elevator," Percival finally answered as he watched the lady walk away.

"Then you must be Mr. Dooley! We were told a young Irish boy named Dooley was attending it!" squealed the pleased couple. Just as Percival turned to escort the couple to his elevator, the lady of his dreams turned quickly around and stared at Percival. What terrible timing! Percival didn't want to walk the couple to his elevator; he wanted to follow the woman of his daily, hourly dreams. But considering he didn't completely see her wide-eyed stare, he walked back toward the V. Nolan with the couple.

But as they began the walk, Percival heard the woman's voice behind him exclaim,

"Dooley?"

He spun around, and she stared another moment. Her eyes from the distance met Percival's as he placed a slight smile upon his face. She then quickly dashed unseen around the corner. This moment was more real than any moment in Percival's life. She couldn't be evil; maybe, he foolishly hoped, she couldn't be a ghost.

Percival's smile and the echo of hearing his name by his dream-lady strengthened him to entertain the couple all the way to Floor 2. "Yes, it came without a ceiling, without a roof!" he shared and beamed as if he owned the elevator.

The workday was almost over. Percival was almost completely plush with Floor 2 and made no effort to perfect it. Mainly because Percival saw, through the glass of the door, his brother Rex standing and waiting for him.

14

A Ghost

"Take me riding," Rex smoothly voiced and ambled in. "Ha! Still in your dancing suit. You saw the girl?" Rex soaked in the decor: the chandelier, the mirror ceiling, the bench. "Yeah... Nice. How high up did you say we can go?" He looked out-of-place appearing in Percival's other world. Rex's strong Irish accent filled the elevator and echoed outside of it, no doubt. Percival shifted his eyes and his stance with a brotherly smirk that felt unfamiliar to his expected work posture. He closed the door and the gate and pulled the lever.

"No, I haven't seen her," he lied. He didn't know why.

"So, we, me brother, hunt the ghost?" Rex offered.

"No, it's not a game, Rex."

"Alright, Percy."

"And, listen, she's not a prop either, Rex."

"Alright, I said."

"She's not a toy, ya' know."

"Then we won't."

"I don't wanna scare her. I don't want her to be scared of me." Percy's eyes were wide. "She's not an evil ghost." He lied again, mostly to himself this time. The brothers stayed uncomfortably silent for at least half a minute.

"Okay," started Percival with a growing smile, "I saw her. Just moments ago. And she heard me name from those guests who just got off the elevator. And ya' know what she did? Ah! She said my name, Rex! 'Dooley?' she said!" Percival's smile was now accompanied with a giggle.

He regained his composure, and he and Rex began upward. The light on Floor 14 shone.

"Try to behave," Percival mumbled.

"What?" answered Rex. Percy stopped flush with the floor, surprising himself. A boy stood waiting, wearing knickers and a newsboy cap. They stared at one another for a moment before the boy inched a foot forward, and then another. He stood between Percival and Rex as the two brothers continued to stare at him.

"I'm meeting Mother to eat," the boy said to Percival.

"The third floor then, in the diner cafe?" Percival asked.

"No, a food banquet or something. The 30th floor, I think Mother told me," he answered. Percival closed the door and gate and began the journey up.

"This meal, lad ... may I accompany you?" Rex asked. The boy didn't answer. He turned back to stare at Percival.

"Sir, is your last name Dooley?"

Percival answered, "Yeah, how d'ya' know that?"

The boy shrugged his shoulders and said, "I just like to know names, you know."

"Mine, dear fellow, is Reginald Dooley. Rex for short. Mr. Percival Dooley there is ten years my junior."

"Oh, you're the brother," the boy said and nodded his head in acknowledgment.

"Well, lad, what is your name?"

The boy turned back to Percival to say, "You're at the 20th floor? I meant Floor 3."

"What?" Percival answered and stopped the elevator to sink back down.

"You're wasting his time, no-name boy! Percy, throw him off!" Rex suggested with no change in his tone.

"Percy?" the boy asked. "Percy Dooley - that's your name."

Percival started the elevator again and said, "I'm not throwing the boy off. He needs his mother."

"I-I see Floor 14 is coming again. I can get off there. Please."

Percival sighed loudly and wished he'd held it in silence. He stopped the elevator at floor 14 and opened the door. The boy walked into the hallway, turned around, and stared at the brothers.

"I like this gate!" exclaimed Rex. "What if we close just the gate ..." Rex closed the gate, leaving the Floor 14 door open. The boy stood and watched.

"No, the guests could fall down the shaft," explained Percival.

"Not at all." Rex disputed. "It's a-"

"Bye, Percy," said a woman's voice. Percival looked up to see where the boy had been standing. It was her, standing on the other side of the closed gate. She smiled at Percival as she walked backwards before turning and leaving.

Percival tried to open the gate too quickly, causing it to lock up. He finally relieved the locked joints of the gate and shoved it open. He leaped into the hallway.

No one.

"It was her," Percival told Rex. "Me- my lady."

"That little boy? This is gravely concerning, Percival—"

"No, Rex—"

A stocky, short woman runs down the hallway shouting, "Wait! Wait!"

"Of course, ma'am!" Percival shouted back. He shifted his feet, thinking. Back to Rex, he explained, "Did she disguise herself? I didn't know."

The short lady, wearing a box hat and a suit dress, scooted her feet to the elevator and turned inside. She panted and held picket signs with "Anti-Saloon League" painted on them. "To the lobby, don't delay!" Percival slid shut the door and the gate and pulled the lever to descend. The elevator seemed to be slower than usual, creeping. *How will I see her again? Just when she lets me? I don't even know when I see her! Perhaps this woman ... No, she couldn't be.* Percival sat on the bench with a slight smile. Rex leaned into the opposite corner but soon took an interest in the new elevator guest.

He asked the lady (which sounded more like a statement than a question), "Where ya going?" The scene shook Percival out of his wistful coma.

The lady resounded like a trumpet, "The protest, of course!"

Percival feared the next words from his brother's mouth.

"Protesting? Where?" Rex asked.

"Somewhere off Broadway Street, south of here." She spurted words quickly, so quickly it juxtaposed with the inching of the elevator. "The entire block swarms at night with drunks and Irishmen, buying liquor instead of their children's food."

Percival watched floor numbers and walls and borders sliding upward as the elevator descended. He studied shadows from Floor 13, unfinished wood trim of Floor 12. Each floor's number floated up slowly like a balloon that didn't really feel like floating anymore. *Please hurry,* Percival thought.

Rex then spoke with a fake American accent and a deeper voice, "The Irishmen!"

Oh, no! thought Percival.

"Children are starving!" swiftly spoke the protester. "And they want to blame the poverty on the stock market. Hah!"

"The devil's drink!" Rex chimed without an iota of his native accent.

Floor 11 most certainly disappeared, and they'd never see it. *Never see it!* The sight of the ghost lady froze in his thoughts. He didn't have a chance to see her long enough. Now he was stuck in a creeping box. Percival stared at the elevator's corner in front of him. The meeting point of the planes and no dust. *Is that angled at exactly 90 degrees?* He wondered. Floor 11 floated away from sight. He huffed out a laugh.

"Have *you* ever drank alcohol?" Rex asked in his fake American accent.

"Well,"

Floor 9, I beg ya', get here! Percival's apathetic face was full of angst. The ghost lady was on the other side of this creeping elevator!

"I drank a small swig out of curiosity from my grandfather's barn decades ago. I didn't care for it. Tasted like gasoline."

"Ah! Ye found the moonshine," Rex's voice of Irish rigor was back. The lady laughed for a moment and then gave a worrisome glance to Rex.

Did it stop? Or is it going backwards? Percival took a deep breath. *It felt like it stopped for a moment there.*

"Are you Irish?" she asked.

"Flowing through me veins, me lady," Rex answered.

"Oh! Dear, sir! I meant no disrespect!" She placed her hand over her chest and didn't know when to close her mouth: "But you know how some of you people are. Not all of you, I'm sure."

"I've no children to me knowing," Rex answered as he rubbed his fingers across the edge of her signs. "I've not yet fallen in love. And dear lady, it makes me want a warm morning brandy."

A fun silence followed.

"Are you in love?" Rex asked the lady. She wouldn't answer. Percival stood his post, facing the wall with amusement obvious on his face, although he wouldn't admit it. "Percy, to the lounge. Me lady needs a warm drink."

"No, thank you," she mumbled out. Then lower, "It's illegal."

"Ah! But in the illegal, me dear lady, is where you find surprises, like love. A small brandy, 'twill loosen ya' up for the protest. And I won't tell anyone!"

Percival witnessed Floor 4 rise taller and taller and lift off. Then, three floors shot off behind it. Percival pulled the lever at Floor 2, a hair too high, but unnoticeable for most. What was noticeable on Floor 2 was how high Luellen's heels were in her thin, tight lavender dress as she pranced towards the elevator holding her cigarette in a long holder.

"Hold it for me, Percy," she called out in a scratchy voice and a grand smile. "Hey ya', Rex." She placed her arms around his neck, and Rex embraced her as well.

The picket sign lady held up a hand balled into a fist with her chin high and exclaimed, "Beware of the coiled serpent!" She offered Percival a shy smile as she exited.

"Me Luellen, baby!" Rex was more fluid than water now, slicker than wax and smoother than velvet. "Stay on the elevator with me all day, huh, doll?"

"Ah, Rex, Sugar. Better yet, you come up to the twenty-fourth floor with me today, sweet cakes. It's an awfully dreadful job. Not a soul to see or talk to all day." They continued hugging and staring at one another. "My boss will be back from Paris in two days, but he's not home yet!" Her statement confused Percival. He was too tired to calculate how Mr. Blaughvoyon could not possibly be in Paris.

"Floor 24, Percy," Rex said without taking his eyes off Luellen. "You heard the lady."

Upon parting from the couple, Percival was alone again. The height between the floor under his feet and the massive, empty space below. He breathed out a laugh; his stress was foolish and irresponsible. He also knew he and the elevator would crash. The outcome was inevitable; he was doomed to fall from heights. Like a faithful pet, the elevator stayed put, ignorant of the danger and stuck in this world of polished decor. The chandelier swayed in a small dance. Percival breathed out another small laugh, thinking of his mother dancing.

As a boy, Percival promised to dance with Mum on her birthday until his father got home from Ireland. The memory gave Percival a smile, but then he remembered the orange dawn each morning beaming behind the protruding buildings. A new day came without his pap. But Percival had no use of giving that memory a solid second. He reassessed his tight surroundings.

One slight jerk of the lever... He took his second potato cake, opened the gate, and saw the endless abyss. He stopped a gasp, bent down to one knee, and dropped his potato cake in between the crack. It charged down out of sight. Percival never heard it land. *Had to have been a soft landing,* he assured himself. It was ridiculous, and it was a secret idiocy that he continued dropping through the elevator cracks.

Perhaps it was the elevator that finally convinced him it knew how to do things, and Percival needed to trust it. Percival pulled the lever of the crank. He had to go down. Everything ends down.

As days passed, Percival acclimated to his post, to uncomfortable passengers, condescending passengers, ghost-like passengers, and to his elevator. As days passed, ups and downs were real, and so were the lives in them.

Occasionally, Charlie stomped into the elevator.

"Pathetic diner!" He mumbled out looking in his large paper bag. "Pathetic. Do they ever get an order right? I'm seriously asking here. Just pathetic." He took out a wrapped sandwich and shoved the bag to Percival. "Here. They gave me an extra sandwich. Apparently, they can't count to one. So, let me out, head to the basement, and eat it."

"Sir, about me paps--"

"He's not here, Dooley. Listen, I need you to hang in there for me. You okay?"

"Yeah."

"Then comb your hair. You need a nice side part. A clean line." He opened the gate himself to get off.

Occasionally, Mr. Hugenby graced himself upon the elevator.

"Dooley," he started, "Take me one floor up as we speak. How's your job faring?"

"As elevator attendant, well, sir," answered Percival. "As for my side duty, I haven't seen her."

"I see. Well, I think you should know she attacked again. The kitchen had a blazing fire last night. It obviously flamed for no reason at all. Had to have been from the ghost. Found no other reason. And we were in great fear of the hotel burning to the ground!"

"Oh, I didn't hear nothing," Percival answered.

"Dooley, you don't know how dangerous she is, and you don't know everything."

"What are ya' talking about, sir?"

"She's like I told you, Dooley, she's a danger," Mr. Hugenby said and rubbed the back of his neck. He exited onto the next floor, each time leaving something for Percival to ponder.

With his next visit, Mr. Hugenby revealed more on the ghost: "She also kills, Dooley. In cold blood. Pure evil. And there's something more that has come to light you need to know — something I've dreaded to tell you." He took out his handkerchief and wiped his forehead with a "my, my" before continuing: "Dooley, we know your father is ... gone. We know because, well, this evil ghost killed your father."

"What are you talking about? My father? What are you talking about?"

Mr. Hugenby placed his puffy hand on Percival's shoulder. "Mr. Blaughvoyon wants you to know, Dooley, how sorry he is to hear of your struggles with no father and- please do not disappoint Mr. Blaughvoyon. Surely you appreciate his kindness... He hopes to see you move up in position here at the hotel. That is, of course, if you do your job." Mr. Hugenby shook Percival's hand before getting off at Floor 3. Percival couldn't speak. He felt his cheeks and forehead redden and burn with a pulse.

Finally, "Sir! Mr. Hugenby!" Percival pleaded. Mr. Hugenby stopped.

"How do you know? What happened? Sir, do you know the whereabouts of my father?"

"Actually, no, Dooley. Only that Mr. Blaughvoyon witnessed the murder, I think."

"What?" Percival shrieked. "Murder? By the woman? I don't understand. Why-"

"By the ghost! She's hardly a woman. More like a monster." Mr. Hugenby stepped closer to Percival. "She badgers and harasses us, taunting us on how she murdered Mr. Dooley- that *was* his last name, wasn't it?" After a quick "yes" from Percival, Mr. Hugenby continued, "She now heckles—"

"I don't understand," Percival voiced. Paps was supposed to be here in the hotel. Or, at least, nearby. A bum in the Chicago alleys. Paps was supposed to be alive, not murdered by the woman of his dreams.

"Heckles," Mr. Hugenby repeated. "She heckles. Like a witch's laugh. Very evil. Anyway, she says, ..." Mr. Hugenby looked behind him down the hallway and back at Percival. "She says the next Dooley is next."

"Next what?"

"Next."

"What happened to me paps?"

"My condolences. Oh, and no, not last night. A long time ago, I do think."

"But then, why do you expect *me* to kill her? She wants to kill me!"

"Dooley, she'll come to you. Right into your hands. She runs from everyone else." Mr. Hugenby turned to leave. "Just stay in your elevator. It's your best weapon. Besides, Mr. Blaughvoyon and I are giving you a chance for revenge. For your own father! Get angry, boy!" He stopped and turned again toward Percival. "Also, Dooley, you have two more days to complete your task. After the said time, you will be relieved from employment here. Lots of bad news, I know. I can't be full of good news all the time." Mr. Hugenby waddled down the hall.

This was not how Percival imagined learning the truth about Mathew Dooley.

For over ten years, Percival and his family guessed, hoped, and dreamed, yet knew nothing. *Where's Pap?* No one knew. Perhaps he'd be home tomorrow ... or then, perhaps tomorrow ... or then, perhaps tomorrow. Now, the miserable truth pressed a weight on Percival, weightier than not knowing. Pap was dead? Percival quickly closed the elevator and sat silently on the bench. His face was warm with despair and tears quickly glazed his face. He thought daily of both possible facts: his father left them for another life, or his father was dead. Neither possibility was heart-breaking until Percival stood in the real one. The chapter of imagining was closed now. And the Ireland holiday was of no use. How would he tell his mother? She was packing and preparing. For nothing. There was nothing to see, no one to see.

Admiration for the ghost lady vanished. He had desired to save her from Mr. Hugenby and Mr. Blaughvoyon — the murderer he dreamed of saving. For the first time, Percival closed the gate with a desire to stay enclosed in his elevator.

He felt like such a fool; he smacked his forehead. *How wretched my mind is! Infested! Stupid, stupid daydreams!* He cursed himself. He felt like a blind man who should have seen something about the beautiful lady that clearly shouted how evil she was. How could he have received no inclination? He scolded himself for daydreaming of kissing her — the woman who killed his father. The knowledge also shook Percival into guilt. He had no loyalty to his leaders or to his job. But now, he would change that. He would find her, remain loyal in his job, and avenge his father's death.

15

A Strange Elevator Encounter

Two days later, a group of well-dressed, diplomatic-looking men stood and spoke a few feet away from Percival and the V. Nolan Elevator. From within the crowd, a man strolled straight into Percival's elevator.

"Do you mind closing it quickly before anyone else comes aboard?" requested the dapper gentleman. Percival obliged and ascended the elevator.

"Hello, Percival Dooley," greeted the stranger. Percival's bewildered look caused the man to chuckle. "Why, you don't know who I am, do you? Perhaps it's best for now considering my humble request to you, sir."

"Sir?" replied Percival who then swallowed. The man was purely American and not an iota of Irish in his blood; these traits Percival instinctively noticed in men around his father's age.

"Have you seen her, Mr. Dooley?" the stranger locked his eyes on Percival's. "The lady."

"Who?" Percival's astonishment rose again. *Surely he doesn't mean the ghost!* thought Percival.

"Marie. She's the ghost here in the hotel. I think, by the look on your face, you have seen her?" Percival said nothing. The moment was too bizarre to utter a sound. Her name was Marie. Marie.

"Surely you're wondering why I am asking? Well, I can tell you. Mr. Dooley, I'm typically a transparent romantic. I'll ..." He cleared his throat before sharing, "I'll tell you — she was my love a few years back. And Marie died here in the hotel. Did you know that?"

Percival shook his head with a whispered "No."

The man continued, "Detectives say she died in her sleep, but she stayed here in the hotel after her death, and I think she's looking for you, Percival Dooley."

Marie. Her name flooded his mind tenderly, and he wished it didn't.

"Who are you, sir?" Percival finally asked.

"In time. For now, know this: *you* are my gift to her, so you're quite valuable to me. Do you understand? She wants to find you, and I want to find her. If she finds you, I will finally find her." The man spoke in a desperate whisper. The elevator stopped. He looked at his watch, straightened up his sports coat, and wrinkled his eyebrows, transforming his romantic side into a stern determination.

"I believe I've said enough for now, Mr. Dooley. Have a good evening." He left the elevator and walked away. Percival remained in the elevator's enclosure, motionless. He felt like he may never leave the encasement of the elevator walls. Only up and back down for poor Percival Dooley.

16

A Crash with a Ghost

Mr. Hugenby was right. Marie would come to Percival. Yet, she wasn't the first woman on his mind when he awoke. He thought of his mother.

The next few mornings, Percival started to speak to Mum, but normal ways, despite how damp and dreary, fell well enough with Lena. He saw how her face's plumpness sat comfortably. He couldn't change things and kill her hope.

"Where's my breakfast? What's going on?" Mr. Wright could be heard in his own home from the Dooley kitchen.

Mrs. Wright scurried back to her home.

Lena fried, sizzled, and simmered potato cakes and a slab of ham. Not a typical morning. Potato cakes were the daily norm and usually were to last for each meal the entire day. Rex brought home the ham — a gift from the Trouers. The aroma traveled throughout the dense neighborhood.

Still catching the ham's aroma, Percival stood in front of the mirror as others used the outdoor lavatory. He felt too timid to shout incoherency. He cupped water in his hands, bent down and slapped his face with the water.

"Yeah, Bua," he proclaimed with composure. The exercise required some warming up. He pooled more water in his hands. His hands looked thin and bony. He splashed the water into an electric smash and wailed, "Bua!"

A boost of life in his core settled his nerves. He repeated the exercise.

"Bua!"

She caused a fire. He'd catch her and save the hotel.

"Bua!"

He would avenge the wrongful death of his father.

"Bua!" It became an eruption of a wail.

Percival entered the kitchen. Lena's moments of sorrow declined; however, a trigger, such as a horseshoe or a Shakespearean sonnet or play stirred Lena's tears. *The Taming of the Shrew* lay open on the table.

In their young years, Mathew introduced Lena to Shakespeare, and *The Taming of the Shrew* was the first play he showed her. He knew what would turn her head to love poetry and reading as much as he did. They laughed through reading the play together, and they read it many times, acting out the parts. Lena played Katherine as despicably as she could, but often broke out laughing. Mathew tried to play the part of a drunken Petruchio, and he delighted Lena as he failed at playing drunk. Lena roared with laughter the day before as she read it, but she laughed alone. Mrs. Wright walked in to inquire about the food sizzling on Lena's stove.

Upon seeing Lena's swollen red eyes and damp face, Mrs. Wright started to leave and stopped beside Percival.

"She's in deep despair. Don't bother her!" Mrs. Wright shouted to Percival from her own house.

"No, I'm quite fine," Lena shook out of her sobbing throat. "Me Mathew! Where'd he go, huh? Where'd he go?" She sobbed in despair.

"Mum," Percival hugged his mother, "you're working too much, Mum. *I'm* going to work. You go to bed."

"Alright," she hugged her son.

"I'm not making your breakfast!" Mrs. Wright screamed. The Dooleys were pleased to hear it.

"I saw a horseshoe in me dream, Percy," Lena shared.

"Ah, Mum. The horseshoe. I saw one recently and thought of Pap.... I gotta go. Try to be happy, for me, Mum?"

Percival received two new potato cakes and began the same morning routine of walking to an internal tune of a lonely whistle, hesitant every four to five steps to ponder:

Did Charlie know his pap was dead?

Was Pap really dead?

Who was the man last night in the elevator?

What else did Mr. Hugenby and Mr. Blaughvoyon know about the ghost lady?

The morning ray bore into his eye, but soon the shadow of the hotel relieved him. As large as it was, it had to have held many, many secrets. They swarmed unseen as he entered the back employee door. Everyone rushed, and so he took post at his elevator, seeing no one to question along the way.

A group of women boarded his elevator for a meeting on Floor 29. They cramped together to make much space away from Percival. He pulled the lever as if he were flying up there himself. The ladies smelled nice of floral perfume, a wonderful scent to fill his small space. At Floor 29, he bade the women a "Good Day" with not a single return, and he started back down.

The light above the elevator door shone for Floor 27. Upon opening the door, Marie, the lady ghost, stood waiting, and she walked onto the elevator. He stared at her for a moment before closing the door and the gate, keeping this moment to himself. The air again changed around him. The elevator even looked different. He was different. He turned and stared at her. She looked like life and all its beauty in every way. His stomach knotted.

"Floor 14, please, Percy," she whispered. He remembered Mr. Hugenby's words.

"Percival?"

"Yeah?" his voice shook.

"Good morning." She smiled. "Are you burdened?"

Percival looked at her, puzzled.

She filled the silence: "I've come close to boarding your elevator once I found out your name."

"Really? What about my name?"

He turned to see her eyes looking up at him. Her eyes were so ivory, and they had another world inside them. He looked away quickly, with a chill.

She was lovely, but he hated her. He had a task. *Her beauty is her tool! She will destroy us!* He heard Mr. Blaughvoyon's voice pleading for Percival to have sense. *She killed your father.* As Percival unwound this truth, he grasped the lever and felt sick. He wanted to flee. He inhaled and stared at the lever. Finally, he pushed the lever and stopped the elevator.

"Percy? What are you doing?" He didn't know how to answer the question. He closed his eyes in hopes this would all be over soon.

"Percy?" Her voice stung his ears. Why did it hurt him so?

No answer. He kept his eyes closed. He was unprepared if she attacked him.

"Is something wrong?... What is it?... Oh, please tell me!"

Percival wanted to avoid the details of his task. It was a simple task, really: stop the elevator and let her die. This part was just testing his endurance. These details were the most tough part of his task. He had to stay focused, so he focused on his pap, whom he never knew and intentionally rarely loved.

"Start the elevator again, please. Please, Percy."

Again, Percy did nothing, standing with his back to her, courageously avenging his father's murder. He held his hands piously together. She lowered to the floor. He thought he heard a cry. She gave quick gasps. Several of them, begging for air.

"Percy,... I can't stay ... in here. I can't breathe.... Percy?"

She was weak and dying, begging him for help. Her pleas were a heavy burden for Percival to hear. "I'm sorry." It wasn't in Percival to ignore a dying woman.

"Percy?... I have something ... to tell ..." She slouched on the floor in the opposite corner. "Percy! ... Percy!" Her voice was beautiful and flooded his heart, but it pierced his ears. The thought dawned on him that she never retaliated. She never attacked him.

"Please, ... Percival..." Her words were faint. The small room became still and quiet. Percival turned to see her trying hard to gasp for air. She then lay motionless.

"No!" Percival shouted as he kneeled beside her lifeless body.

He placed his hand on the lever and pulled. Marie suddenly gasped again softly for air. The sound of her suffering ignited him to pull the lever to the next door. However, upon pulling the lever, the elevator returned a strange reek. It then fell quickly, plummeting for a solid length of fright before stopping. The elevator tilted and jarred in the shaft. The ghost remained slouched on the floor. Her weak eyes revealed the ivory color. She panted.

"What have you done?" Percival asked the ghost. "You're trying to kill me, too!" Percival acknowledged

"What do you mean?" she was still on the floor, trying to regain strength. The elevator strained with moans and creaks.

"You did this! Why? Why'd you kill me Pap?" The elevator groaned in reply.

The ghost said nothing else. She lowered her head to hide her eyes once again. She held on to the guardrail and steadied her feet into a stance. The top corner dropped more. Percival thought the end of his life was certain with one more creak. One more moan. He huffed quick breaths.

A meow caught their attention. Percival saw that Floor 15's door was reachable.

"Who told you I killed your father?" the ghost asked. "It's not true."

A second meow hummed from behind the Floor 15 door. Percival gently and slowly slid his feet to reach the gate and inch it open. As he gasped for breath, he reached up to grab the bottom of the door. The elevator creaked and fell more sideways, leaving a smaller amount of the door in sight. With a stretched arm, he strained to push open the heavy door. It barely moved. He looked over to see the ghost plastered to the other side of the elevator. The cat looked at Percival and Marie and greeted them with a *meow*. The elevator moaned.

"Can you float, by chance?" Percival asked her.

"No."

"Then, step on me and hoist yourself through the door as soon as I push it open. Ready?"

"No! It might fall more!"

"Then why are you doing this?" demanded Percival.

"I have nothing to do with this!" answered the ghost.

Percival stared in admiration at the ghost's insecurity, vulnerability, and maybe even her need for him. He reached up to the door. The elevator grunted. Beads of sweat ran down his face. He pushed with his stretched arm to open the sliding door. Finally, it opened.

"Grab my hand and climb up the handrail!" He offered his long, bony hand to Marie. "You can trust me." In receiving her hand, Percival noticed it had a cloud-like surface. The core of the mass of her hand grasped his hand back. She quickly made her way up, surprising Percival. He could now only see her shoes, but he heard her voice.

"Thank you, Percy. I must go. The hotel seems to like you." She bent down, leaving an earring beside the cat. Percival then watched her shoes run away. He stepped closer toward the opened exit. The elevator jolted down more, leaving less space for him to get out. He stood frozen in the elevator for several minutes. He then heard footsteps coming closer. A man's footsteps came right above Percival's head. Percival was hidden from the man's sight.

"Good kitty," he heard the man whisper, picking up the meowing cat and the earring. Then, the footsteps walked away.

Percival lifted himself to the door, surprised by his own strength. He squeezed through the small opening. He stood up on Floor 15. Marie nor anyone else was in sight. She was gone again. The earring was gone. He wanted to faint. He sat in the hallway, and soon a group of men dashed to the opened elevator door beside Percival.

Percival stumbled in exhaustion and searched for Mr. Hugenby.

"She tried to kill you, too!" Mr. Hugenby exclaimed to Percival. "The elevator is jarred at a tilt, bound to fall any second!"

Hugenby's eyes grew enormous, and his face reddened and puffed up. He fled in titter-totter steps down the hallway, his hands out by his sides as if he was looking for a dance partner.

Feeling lightheaded, Percival, encouraged by Mr. Hugenby, resorted to the employee locker room. Percival slouched in a plastic chair and stared at the floor, too mentally drained to think of anything but the clean, dull cement floor, letting his eyes rest on it. His motionless body succumbed to sleep.

"Hello? Hello? Wake up, will ya'?" Hubert Downey shouted and stood over Percival. Trying to regain coherency, he stared up at Hubert.

"They're lookin' for you everywhere, Dooley, mad as hell, too. Something about a rat infestation and a pile of pancakes. And you and I both know who those are from, don't we?"

Percival mumbled in confusion.

"Look, the Union is gonna have a tough time with this one, but it's all ya' gotta say — 'The Union's handling it.' Then, they'll shake in their rich-boy boots." Hubert offered a hand to help Percival up. "I got chewed out myself. For accepting a guest invitation — that's what they called it. It was just some girls. Invited me into their room. What single, good-lookin' guy says no to that?" Hubert dusted off Percival's back once he was finally standing. "Ya' look awful. Listen, get cleaned up. Quick. Big cheese wants to see you. Now."

"Big cheese?" asked Percival.

"Mr. Blaughvoyon himself. They said he just flew in from Paris."

"In his penthouse? On Floor 24?"

"Is that where it is? Well, well. But no, uh, just go to his office on Floor 2."

Percival washed his face. Hubert left the room and shouted, "Don't take any wooden nickels. And don't forget: the Union's handling it!"

With a heavy weight of too many things to think about, Percival found the door on Floor 2: "The Office of Nicholas Blaughvoyon." He knocked just as Mr. Hugenby approached him.

"Never mind, Dooley. No need to bother him now. Go home for the day and rest. See you in the morning."

"Thank you, sir."

They both turned to walk away when the office door opened. A man in a suit held the door open and asked, "Percival Dooley?" Percival paused and looked back at Mr. Hugenby before joining the man.

"Wait!" shouted Mr. Hugenby. He shuffled back toward Percival, stood behind him, and took him by the shoulders. "We should continue this first thing in the morning. Mr. Dooley has suffered great trauma and should go home right away."

"I demand to see him now, Button!" a man's voice called from a deeper room. Percival recognized the man's voice, but it wasn't Mr. Blaughvoyon's.

"Yes," Mr. Hugenby answered. "I understand. Well, I'll attend as well." Mr. Hugenby started into the doorway.

"Button, we'll inform you later. Just Mr. Dooley for now." Mr. Hugenby excused himself to "attend to hotel matters."

He turned around and whispered to Percival, "Don't believe what they say. Something strange is going on here."

Percival walked into the office where a man stood up from behind his desk and held out his hand to shake. The man was the stranger Percival met in the elevator the night before, the dapper gentleman who knew Marie.

Charlie leaned against a bookshelf and said, "How ya' doing, Percy?"

"Good day, Mr. Dooley. I'm Nicholas Blaughvoyon. My hotel team knows me as either Nick or Mr. B. You may call me either that suits you. I've actually been looking forward to meeting with you again, but not in this reprimanding manner."

"You're ... who?" asked Percival, still standing.

Mr. Hugenby was correct; something wasn't right.

"Sit down, Percival. I'm not repeating all that. I own this hotel. Let's get down to business. Are you responsible for—"

"No, wait, but—you're *not* Mr. Blaughvoyon," interrupted Percival. Percival didn't appreciate being lied to.

The supposed Mr. Blaughvoyon's eyes grew wide. He chuckled. "I'm quite sure of most identities in my hotel this very second, and I'm certain of my own. Why would you declare such a thing?"

"Well, I already met Mr. Blaughvoyon. You're not him."

"Mr. Dooley, you met me, yes, in the elevator just yesterday. You don't remember?"

"Yes, but no. I met Mr. Blaughvoyon. Just a few weeks ago. On my first day of work."

"You must have met a different Blaughvoyon, or you were mistaken."

"No. No mistake. Mr. Blaughvoyon introduced himself to me."

"As Nicholas Blaughvoyon?"

"Yes, the owner of this hotel."

"I'm the owner of this hotel."

"Sir, no, the Blaughvoyon I met was the owner of this hotel. You're not him."

With a stern stare, the man replied, "Are you mad? I should sue you for the damage you've done to my hotel. It's your choice: termination with a lawsuit you can't afford or we can have a sensible discussion. Have I made myself clear!" Percival stared in bewilderment and sat slowly. He didn't know where he was in the hotel, perhaps the part of the mind where all the secrets were kept.

The man continued, "Where did you meet this other Blaughvoyon man? It's not common to do so, so forgive me if I have as difficult a time believing you as you have me. Where did you meet him?"

"I met him in his penthouse. In the North Wing on Floor 24. So, you can't be him."

"Your first day of employment, you said? On your crew's first day of work, I was in Paris. You didn't meet me."

A memory of Luellen's words flashed back to Percival: "... *I thought he was in Paris... I've never seen him.*" A large photograph hung on the wall beside where Percival sat. The picture showed the man presently claiming to be Mr. Blaughvoyon smiling and cutting a ribbon with a crowd around him. Another photo showed the man standing outside the hotel with other men.

"I'm confused. You're Nicholas Blaughvoyon?" Percival stared at Mr. Blaughvoyon as if he was a ghost. Mr. Blaughvoyon's eyes pointed at photos of himself framed on the wall. Some backgrounds of the photos were inside the hotel.

"Again, yes. Did someone else claim to be me?"

Percival was still confused and sat back. He asked, "You're Mr. Blaughvoyon?"

"Who claimed to be me, Mr. Dooley? Did someone else claim to be me? Did you take orders from this person?"

"Yes, in the penthouse."

"The new crew was introduced to this person as Mr. Blaughvoyon?"

"No, just me in a private meeting."

"What floor was that you said?"

"The twenty-fourth floor, sir."

"That penthouse is not even fully furnished. You were there? The north wing of that entire floor is being renovated. Charlie," Mr. Blaughvoyon began.

Percival faced Charlie and asked, "You are really Charlie?"

Charlie smiled with one corner of his lips and answered, "Yeah, kid. It's me. And I didn't plan for you to meet an imposter."

"Mr. Dooley," asked the supposedly real Mr. Blaughvoyon, "do you know Charlie?"

"I found him and hired him, Nick," Charlie answered.

The supposedly real Mr. Blaughvoyon smiled wide and said to Charlie, "Hah! Of course you did! Charlie, find out who's been on the twenty-fourth floor."

"Sir, Mr. Hugenby, my manager, introduced me to Mr. Blaughvoyon, or to someone who said he was you?" said Percival. He noticed that his voice didn't shake at all. He wasn't the least bit nervous of speaking to a man in power because he wasn't convinced this man had power.

"Who was the man with my name?" asked Mr. Blaughvoyon. His face turned weightier. He led a silence in the room, as uncomfortable as silences can be. "Describe the man who claimed to be me."

Mr. Blaughvoyon's face reddened with his jaw clinched. Mr. Blaughvoyon—or, the man claiming to be Mr. Blaughvoyon, perhaps the second Mr. Blaughvoyon, looked rich. His skin was a pleasant tan, not too dark. His brown wavy hair, neither too thick nor too thin, was long enough to tell it was wavy and tactfully in place. He wore a dark blue ascot around his collar, tucked into his dark gray vest under his dark gray jacket. Nothing was too loose and nothing too tight. Nothing too dark and nothing too light. The only extreme about this man, whoever he was, was his detailed appearance of perfection.

"He's a tall man. With a twisty, twirly mustache."

Mr. Blaughvoyon's eyebrows deepened with concern. He said, "I'll handle this. For now, we need to set this matter aside. Mr. Dooley, we need to discuss the reason you're here. You need to know that a scatter of pancakes—"

"Potato cakes—um, perhaps."

"Identity is extremely important to you, I see, despite however construed." Charlie and the other men in the office sang out a short, laughing cadence. "Potato cakes on top of a pile of hotel pillows lay under your assigned elevator. Do you know why? Did the fake Mr. B tell you to do it?"

Percival remained quiet, wanting to conjure an air-tight lie about how the kitchen staff must have thrown them in there. No, perhaps —

"Answer me or you're fired."

He must be the real Mr. Blaughvoyon! thought Percival. "I can't say for sure. But I think the vagrant bums have found a way in and sleep there on cold nights. I saw a ragged man come out of the pit once. I greeted him with hospitality, but I could tell he wasn't a guest and he wasn't a worker. He ran off scared, straight out the kitchen's back door." Percival felt accomplished. He refrained from admitting his fear and definitely from his potato-cake droppings.

Mr. Blaughvoyon stared with deep apathy and spoke, "A rat or two found the pan—potato cakes — and invited a thousand of their rat friends. The uncivilized rodents came into my hotel and chewed on a steel rope that controlled the suspension. Keep in mind, Mr. Dooley, this elevator, the V. Nolan, which is now at risk of being destroyed, is the golden core of the hotel. It was built in 1892. You were placed in charge of this gem. An investigation is underway."

The potato cakes caused the elevator wreck, not the ghost, not the woman who changed the air around Percival into golden peace. Marie. He himself caused the elevator to fall and become jarred in the shaft. He let her come close to dying, if a ghost can die a second time.

But even though she didn't try to kill Percival, the fact remained that she killed Percival's father.

"Mr. Dooley, you said you met privately with these men. Were you given a particular assignment? What was it?"

He enlightened Mr. Blaughvoyon's curiosity: "To catch a ghost."

"My God, no," Mr. Blaughvoyon proclaimed.

A meow sounded under the desk, and the old calico cat climbed into Mr. Blaughvoyon's lap. Chills covered Percival's body.

Mr. Blaughvoyon ordered all other men present to leave his office, all but Percival.

17

Mr. Nicholas Blaughvoyon

It wasn't that Percival ever bonded and befriended the cat, but now he wondered if the cat was a traitor. Who was it truly loyal to? It sat contently in the lap of the secondly identified Nicholas Blaughvoyon, cuddled as if it had done this many times.

Nicholas' face softened as he looked at Percival.

"I wasn't expecting you to answer that question. Not as you did," Nicholas began. "I also know why Button placed you there with the V. Nolan. He placed you there because Charlie told him to. Most guests prefer the more modern elevators, so she would probably take yours."

"Who would take the elevator?"

"Marie was with you on the elevator today?"

"Yes," Percival answered, "but Mr. Hugenby ordered me to find her and trap her."

Nicholas looked away and placed his fist in front of his mouth. "Atrocious!" Which part disturbed Nicholas the most as atrocious — the ghost, the cat, Mr. Hugenby's ghost-catching orders, the fake Mr. Blaughvoyon, or the crashed elevator — Percival wasn't certain. Yet his gestures seemed genuine and compassionate, and Percival liked him. He told Nicholas of the ghost and her evil works of danger and horror throughout the hotel. Percival shared with Nicholas of the ghost's murder of his own father.

"Button knows of your father's death?" Nicholas replied in a startle. "How does *he* know?"

"The man who said he was you knows. Mr. Hugenby gave me the message from him," Percival immediately retorted, feeling heat burn on the back of his neck.

Nicholas quietly pondered with small murmurs of "Puzzling" and "A mystery" as he petted his cat. He opened a desk drawer and placed a black box on his desk. He reached inside his coat pocket and pulled out Marie's earring, the one she left on the Floor 15 hallway floor. Inside the box was a collection of ladies' accessories: such things as a lady's black silk glove, a letter opener, a feather from a hat, and a napkin with a lipstick blot. He reached down to pick up a black glove from the floor where the cat had been sitting.

"Thank you, ole' cat!" Nicholas chuckled. "I now have the pair. She might be missing these." He admired the collection of Marie's things, stolen from the calico cat or left to find by Marie.

"Marie herself told me about your father's death, Mr. Dooley, when she was still living. My sincerest condolences, but she didn't kill your father. Furthermore, you are relieved of Mr. Hugenby's orders, but not mine. Like I told you in the elevator — you were brought here as a gift to Marie. Now, lead me to Marie."

Percival wondered if Mr. Hugenby was truthful. *"Believe nothing they tell you!"* he told Percival.

"Lead me to Marie."

"Marie?"

"She has more to tell you. It's not for me to say."

Nicholas explained his orders to meet in a second south wing elevator on Floor 14 later in the evening.

"And, Mr. Blaughvoyon," began Percival, "do you want to hurt Marie as well?"

"Are you yourself wanting to hurt poor Marie, Mr. Dooley?" Nicholas tightened his lips.

"No! I meant 'as well as Mr. Hugenby'!"

This cleared the confusion and softened Nicholas' face. "Did Button tell you why he wants to hurt Marie?"

"Yes, because she's dangerous is what he told me."

Nicholas bid Percival farewell and waited for Percival to close the door behind him before collapsing his face of anguish into his hands.

18

Plots of Percival

The Union is on your side, my friend!" Hubert shouted to Percival across the lobby, standing firm as if ready for battle. Percival glanced sideways for onlookers and walked toward him.

"So, did ya' get canned? Mr. Dapper with his pretty hair in there? That was phonus balonus, I tell ya'."

"Yeah, but I didn't get canned. Have you ever seen Mr. Blaughvoyon?" asked Percival.

"He grilled me earlier about the invitation I got from the pretty girls. But ya' know what? You just say 'Union' and they're all balled up. The dames are on Floor 17," Hubert turned and smiled at Percival. "I think I'd like to say hello."

Before he closed his elevator, Percival asked, "Have you seen Mr. Hugenby?"

"Yeah, the slimeball got on Claude's elevator a while ago," Hubert said. "I don't like 'em. Somethin' 'bout 'em I don't like." A group of ladies dressed in dinner gowns walked into

Hubert's elevator. "Wanna go with us?" he asked Percival, who shook his head with a nervous smile and backed away.

"Alright, but you're dusting out at a crazy time." Hubert gave his attention to the girls. "Which of you tomatoes got a gasper for your favorite guy Hubert?"

The V. Nolan elevator was blocked with a rope and a sign: "Temporarily Out of Order." From the outside of the V. Nolan, it looked solid and capable. As he looked at the V. Nolan entryway, his mind grappled with what was true. Mr. Hugenby was a good boss, wasn't he? Percival's head swirled. Why did he mention his father? Thoughts of the horseshoe on the penthouse wall flashed in his thoughts.

Percival changed out of his uniform, left the hotel, and walked to Trouer Tower. His mind was young and strong, and the mechanics of the sixteen-year-old mind which has rambled in and out of other realms and crashed elevators and penthouses and offices of the CEO work seamlessly. Each step became more confident as he stirred his thoughts into a plan. Plans of this sixteen-year-old Irish boy were, whether a success or a failure, always extremely dangerous. A small space between buildings showed Lake Michigan reflecting the sky, trying to close the day. The sun wasn't bright anymore. He glared through the window. Rex saw him and came out.

"Did ya' hear that? The General's shoutin' for justice," Rex came out and lit a cigarette.

"The ghost?" Percival asked.

"Yeah, he wants a pint. *Gimme my bloody pint!* Do ya' hear his British gab?" Rex gave a large, open-mouth smile and laughed. Percival couldn't hear anything over Rex's laugh.

"Hey," Percival looked around, "somebody's playing dirty, maybe."

"Sounds fun," Rex answered. "You wanna come in for a drink? Wyatt and me, we finished cleaning," Rex emphasized, pointing at Percival. "And I'm starting a new tight-roping business, Percy. Customers can walk from building to building on a tightrope right here in Chicago. It's the new thing. In the 1930s, it's how people will travel."

"What if they fall?"

"Yeah, I'm still smoothing out the details. You wanna drink?"

"No, no. Rex, my elevator crashed today." Rex paused his walk and stared in dismay at Percival, who was still alive, but his luck was diminishing. But he was still alive. Percival didn't mention the potato cakes; he didn't blame Rex nor himself. Percival was destined to fall, no matter the caveats. It was fate.

There would never be a good time to mention their father, and Percival pondered this before releasing: "Pap may not be living anymore. "

They walked in silence.

"You're a depressing fellow this evening, Percy. It's the ghost girl, isn't it? She got you down."

Percival explained the information he received from Mr. Hugenby and the real Mr. Blaughvoyon.

"That is …" Rex shook his head and scrunched his lips under his mustache, "not true."

"I hope you're right, but Mr. Blaughvoyon says the ghost will tell me everything."

"A dirty trick it sounds like! Playing dirty! How do they know? I'll bust 'em!" Rex gritted his teeth. As they walked, Rex carried a grave look and breathed deeper. He added, "I wanna see Pap one more time, me brother, at least one more time." His head seemed weighed down, preventing him from looking up. Rex said so many times for several years.

"Yeah, I hope you do; we do."

"I'd rather Pap be a rotten low-life than dead, ya' know?" Rex shared, but Percival couldn't relate with much depth. He never knew Pap. His relationship with Pap was based on stories and memories from others.

"I want to see him, too," Percival expressed and breathed out a small laugh followed with a frown. The brotherly bond sealed tighter. "And Rex, this trick, or somethin'—it's not fun, Rex. They speak about Pap, and two different men tell me they're the real Mr. Blaughvoyon. One of 'em says the ghost is his girl. I want her to be *my* girl."

Percival explained how he should have noticed the emptiness of the penthouse on Floor 24, the first day he met someone claiming to be Mr. Blaughvoyon. "But I just thought — maybe that's how rich people live. How was I supposed to know?" The poverty of the Dooleys comprised clutter, houses squeezed in beside others. All his neighbors and acquaintances were poor, as proved by the things all around them. Mud and puddles everywhere mixed with trash, a stick or two, a spoon, a clay pot, a blanket coated in brown, odds and ends, and maybe a shoe. His home was stuffed with his mother's collections and whatever they were given or found for cheap at the market: a candelabra, a jar, a broken basket, a stool, a stack of papers. Mathew Dooley kept stacks of books, and Lena kept them all. The only empty space in their home was on the wall where the horseshoe once hung. Seeing empty space indoors was believed to have meant the opposite of the Dooleys — rich.

"A horseshoe was all the penthouse had hanging on the wall; now isn't that weird," Percival said and looked around him again. He laughed to himself at the thought and continued, "Why, Rex? Out of all things, why did they hang a horseshoe in the penthouse?"

"Is it still hanging there?" Rex asked.

"As far as I know," Percival continued.

"They say when something feels like home, me brother, it's yours," Rex said.

"What? Who says that? Nobody says that but a thief. But I tell ya', me thoughts went directly to Pap when I saw it, and I'm willing to steal it."

Rex looked to the right and left and said, "Let's take it. The horseshoe. Listen," Rex stepped closer to Percival, still looking around, "I'll go to the hotel to see Luellen. I'll get her to let me in there. I gotta see this thing."

"Alright, let's go."

"No, just me. You'll get us kicked out."

"I have to meet Mr. Blaughvoyon later tonight. I have to go, too." Rex studied Percival as Percival stared off wistfully.

"What's the lady ghost's name, Percy?" Rex calmed his brother.

"Marie." Percival's smile died. He was just an Irish boy, but perhaps Mr. Blaughvoyon was evil, and Percival would save Marie from his wicked schemes. Percival hoped Mr. Blaughvoyon was evil. He hoped he was a liar and a hater of the Irish. Percival couldn't be a hero amidst the good and powerful. He couldn't have Marie to himself.

"Gimme a few minutes to kiss Luellen and hug her several times. And I'll see you there."

Just as Rex prepared to part, an automobile stopped beside them. Mrs. Wright blasted open the door and jumped out, shouting at the Dooley brothers. "Get in with me! We must help my husband! Those filthy children again! Get in the car!" she ordered. If "filthy children again" were involved, Mr. Wright injured himself chasing children off their roof. He'd throw and hit every child he could catch.

"Or let him die, Mrs. Wright. Be free, woman," answered Rex.

"Love your neighbor! ... Percy?" she ordered more than asked.

"Percy is at your service," offered Rex. With that, she crawled back into the car. Rex gave Percival a pushed pat on the back and waltzed toward the hotel.

"Mrs. Wright," began Percival, bent over to see in the car window, "I'm afraid I can't"-

"Get in!"

Mr. Wright yanked the small medicine bottle from Mrs. Wright.

"Just a teaspoon at a time, the doctor told me," instructed Mrs. Wright. Mr. Wright cursed her and the bottle before turning it up and drinking the entire bottle. He reclined back and was quickly out.

"Is he dead?" asked Percival. "Poisoned?"

"Certainly not, stupid boy!"

Percival would never introduce Marie to Mrs. Wright. She'd embarrass him.

Upon entering his home, he noticed open spaces where clutter had always dwelt. His mother came in the door behind him.

"Heavens, Percy! Ya' got fired already, didn't ya'?" she asked. "I'm clearing out old stuff, doing me part, I am. But if ya' get no money, we get no Ireland. Then, we never find Mathew. Don't ya' see, me boy!' Her voice escalated.

"I'm not fired, Mum. I'm not." A sadness settled in his chest.

Lena opened the hope chest and pulled out a thick plastic bag. She revealed the dress her husband had bought her years ago. Under the dress lay a horseshoe.

"Maybe just a little tight now."

"I'll take you to dinner, Mum, as soon as I get me work pay."

"Such a sweet boy. I can take meself if Mathew won't. One day."

"Whose horseshoe?" Percival asked and took the horseshoe from the chest.

"Me sights! Ah, it's nothin'! Me stole it from a stable barn outside Chicago some years ago. I don't know why I did. A cat was scratching away at it strangely. Just caught me eye." She put away the dress and tended to another pile.

"Can I keep it for tonight, Mum?"

"Alright, but Percy, there's no luck in it. I stole it, I told ya'!"

Percival soon made his way back toward the hotel. He had a knot in his chest and uneasiness in his stomach, but he pushed his feet forward. Everyone wanted Marie — one to kill her, one to love her, or so he said. Percival thought of stealing Marie to save her. He'd take her away from the hotel. He'd take her to Ireland. The attributes of her beauty overcrowded the attributes of the ghost.

The South Wing elevator sat in a drab, quiet end of a hallway. Few guests visited this area of the hotel. However, the elevator was modern and easier to operate than the V. Nolan. Percival stood alone in the elevator with a swarm of thoughts. Was Percival merely the bait for this new Nicholas Blaughvoyon? He had time to flee; he thought about it too long. Nicholas soon appeared. They paused and stared for a moment before Nicholas boarded the elevator.

"How will she know to come to this elevator?" Percival broke the silence.

"She'll know," Nicholas answered. His face was younger-looking and brighter. Percival felt of less worth. In no time, they heard a meow, and Marie appeared with the slow-moving calico cat in front of her. She locked her surprised eyes with Nicholas. He gasped at the sight of her cloudy white eyes. He grabbed his chest and breathed deeply. Marie gave no acknowledgment of Percival, and Percival noticed, refraining from grabbing his own chest. Percival wanted to stare at her, but Nicholas's reaction surprised him.

"I was devastated," Nicholas began between deep breaths, "devastated upon hearing you were gone." Nicholas struggled to get his breath. He glanced over at Percival and tried to calm down before continuing. "I've missed you terribly."

"Nick," answered Marie, "I've missed you, too, but I can't be everything. Not anymore."

Percival's heart was coated dull. He pushed a button and closed the door. Many doors closed.

"Where shall we go?" Percival interrupted the couple's moment.

"Nowhere for a moment," Nicholas stated as he stared at Marie.

"Up, Percy," answered Marie. "As far up as we can go."

"I was determined to carry out your mission. Why you came here to Chicago," Nicholas stated. He explained how he often had employment sign-ups outside, waiting for a Dooley to apply. He ordered hotel management to hire Percival if they ever came across his name. Carrying out the "mission" wasn't Nicholas's mission at all; he wanted only to find Marie for himself. And what was this mission? How was Percival the means? Percival had questions, but Marie chimed in first.

"I'm sorry—"

Percival interrupted Marie, "Do you know where my father is?"

19

A Ghost Story

Marie stared at Percival like a child waiting for permission. "Up, please," she said.

"He knows nothing, sweet Marie," Nicholas said to her. "He should like to hear you tell him everything."

Falling was not a thought, but if Percival never truly felt pushed aside, he was about to. An unfortunate start to their meeting. It was more than a twenty-year-old man could take, much less a sixteen-year-old boy, much less a boy pushed aside in the air destined to fall.

"How far up?" Percival asked. The moment was quiet; Percival's aggravation was palpable.

"Floor 31, Mr. Dooley," Nicholas said and looked at Marie. "Our ballroom," he lowered his voice.

At Floor 31, in a dark, empty, palatial ballroom, Percival remained like a vulnerable victim. His eyes were enormous. He waited beside Marie as Nicholas searched for lights and secured the doors. The forgotten ballroom was cold.

Percival gazed at Marie and felt tranquil. His only burden was blinking and missing something. He didn't forget the world around him nor the distress of his situation; but more importantly to him, he remembered the world around them as nothing but space without the one he loved being beside. She quieted his mind. The rest of the world stood as still as they did.

"Percival Dooley," she stated, as if confirming his name rather than admiring it.

The ghost paused and stared as if frightened of what Percival would find in her eyes. A chandelier on the far side of the ballroom suddenly brightened its area. Nicholas sat at a distance in the ballroom. Marie looked over at Nicholas as if for affirmation. She breathed in deep and tried to steal a smile or two despite her face enraptured in dread.

"Yes? Please, miss." Percival stepped closer and became surrounded within her ivory eyes. White waves leaped deep in her eyes. The color quickly dimmed and a dense dust occupied the white space. But her eyes were void of life although they clearly looked at him, and they frightened Percival.

"My name is Marie-Louise Chadoir. I am from France." She lowered her face and eyes.

Her lovely accent lulled Percival's discomfort. He basked in the sounds of her words which filled the surrounding air over the darkness above him. He strangely felt as if his feet were levitating.

"Tell me everything. Why are you not alive? Are you? Have you ever been? Who are you?"

She took one of his hands and led him to sit with her. "I grew up in France with my parents, and I worked as an infirmière in our home. We lived by the Deûle River in the city of Lille.

"Maisons in Lille, oh, they were so stuffy and so hot, swarming with germs. Sick patients came to me, but we were poor like everyone else. They paid when they could, maybe a franc a month. Then my own Maman and Papa grew ill, probably from germs I brought into our home. A friend, a médecin said they were too sick to survive. He gave them médicament for a peaceful sleep, and neither of my parents ever woke up again.

"I miss them. They were my best friends, so I know how precious — I wanted to go far away, tired of France, its darkness.

"So, everyone in Lille was excited about the news of the Titanic, of the giant ship heading for America. The Titanic was coming to Cherbourg! I secured a ticket and boarded as a nurse. I was assigned to work with the other médecins, with doctors from England, too."

Percival enjoyed hearing of Marie's past, but he bowed his head and waited to hear about his father. Marie studied him and continued, "The first evening on board, we met the most repulsive drunk, slouched in his own vomit on a bench — Mr. Lymon Braham," Marie enunciated his name with anger. "Even when he was sober, he was loud and rude.

"The hôpital crew slept and ate when we could, many times after guests had already eaten. On my first night aboard the ship, I ate at a table alone. Most of the dining room was empty, and a man was cleaning tables. He started to sway, losing his balance, and I could tell he was feeling seasick.

"I rushed to him and made him sit down," Marie said. "I had him tell me all about himself so as to forget his nervous stomach. He told me he was going home. To Chicago. His name was Mathew Dooley."

Percival's heart felt full. His eyes grew hungry and wide, staring at Marie.

"My father was on the Titanic? Where is he? … Oh, no." He gasped and let go of a tear. He begged Marie, "Please, what else? You spoke to my Pap?" Another tear streamed down Percival's face.

"Percival, yes, I met your dear father," she began with smiling eyes. "He had a thick, deep Irish accent, and he said he wished he had his horseshoe in his pocket so he'd stop feeling sick, but he left it in his quarters. Such a lovely Irish accent he had! He told me he had two sons, and one he would meet for the first time when he arrived home. He spoke of his wife and his love for her. The next day, I saw him with half of a horseshoe sticking out of his pocket."

Percival breathed out a small laugh.

Marie abruptly stopped smiling. "The next time I saw him was at the sinking. So many people were screaming and crying on the ship, wandering where their husbands were, where their children were."

"Oh, me Pap!" Percival whispered. He heard Marie's voice in his head, crying.

"I saw your father. I saw him walking and trying to smile, and oh, how I hurt for his family, waiting for him in America!" Her cry escalated.

"He saw me staring at him, and he walked up to me and smiled. I will never forget his words. They are etched in my memory forever." As she proceeded, Percival could hear a second voice paired with Marie's voice. It was the voice of his Pap, the voice of Mathew Dooley: "Drowning is not such a bad way to die! Immersed in something so beautiful. Breathing in the forbidden. It becomes part of you. So, when you see me wife — her name is Lena — tell her I died most romantically. Tell me boys I love 'em!"

"That was me Paps."

"Percy, your father thought nothing of himself. He knew I was scared as the ship was sinking. He was trying to help me deal with dying in the water."

After some reflection, Marie continued.

"A lifeboat called for me to leave the ship and jump aboard to help an injured man. People were shouting in the water everywhere. I was horrified! Then I heard the voice of the drunkard Mr. Braham say, 'Get over it! We can't feel bad for not dying!' He was in the same boat as I. Suddenly, a man panting for breath swam to the boat and begged Mr. Braham to pull him inside. Mr. Braham shouted, 'There's no room! Die with some dignity, not like a beggar!' The man held on to the edge of the boat, and I saw his face better — it was Mathew Dooley!"

"No," Percival responded softly and hung his head.

"I shouted for the men to let him in, but no one would listen to me. Mr. Dooley held his horseshoe. Mr. Braham told him, 'There's only room for your horseshoe, you vagrant!' With that, Mr. Braham jerked to pull the horseshoe out of Mr. Dooley's hand, but Mr. Dooley's grip was tight. He clung to it, letting his own body swim with one arm. When Mr. Braham finally snatched it, your father was gone."

Percival lowered his head and clinched his jaw.

"I'm so sorry," Marie-Louise added.

Percival placed his face in his hands and wept. The hotel stood silent in reverence — not a door, not an elevator, not a light switch moved. Marie remained quiet for a very long time as well.

"Percy, there's more you must know. Once I finally reached the mainland of the States, the words of your father bore a heavy weight upon me. My mission was to find Chicago and find the Dooleys."

Marie explained the years before she arrived in Chicago. She needed money and food, so she settled in Boston for a few years. When she expressed her mission to a doctor she worked for, he eventually gave her the money needed to board a bus and stay at a ritzy hotel. She was then on her way to find Lena, Rex, and Percival Dooley.

The Blaughvoyon Hotel came with many surprises, one being the quickly grown affection she shared with Nicholas Blaughvoyon. During their relationship, she shared with Nicholas her reason for being in Chicago.

"It's a good hotel, a luxury dream hotel, but it can get sick. In the hotel guest lounge, I met eyes with the murderer himself—Mr. Lyman Braham! He was employed here at the hotel. I was more mortified in my live body than I am now in this dead one. I came here to offer peace, and this murderer walked freely!"

"Braham? The same guy who murdered Paps!" said Percival.

"Yes, I wanted to find Nicholas right away and tell him. Mr. Braham saw me and must have remembered me. He—he smiled at me. I was disgusted! I couldn't hide it. He followed me on an elevator, your assigned elevator, so I quickly got off. He followed me down the hallway. So, I got on the stairwell. I climbed many flights of stairs before slowing down. He followed me, shouting that he'd catch me. And then he did.

"He came behind me on the steps and grabbed me. His arms squeezed me. I tried to scream, but I couldn't. He smelled of liquor and rotting flesh. Suddenly, I felt strong, and I pushed him off me. He fell backward, and he must have become disoriented. He leaned sideways, stumbled, and rolled over the railing and off the stairwell. I could hear the bangs and cracks of the rails of each floor as he fell from a floor to a deeper floor. Falling, and then a horrible thud. The whole stairwell felt evil and dark. He was dead."

"But my dear," Nicholas began; he stood and walked toward Marie, "What happened to you?"

"Yes, I haven't revealed my own death yet to anyone. And even though I'm here to reveal the truth of Mathew Dooley, my own murder must also be told."

Nicholas cooed over Marie, stating, "Murder! I knew it!" He embraced her before she retook her seat on the couch beside Percival.

"I was free, or so I thought. I climbed to Floor 14 and opened the door into the hallway. Mr. Button Hugenby — a man I didn't know at the time — stood in front of me in the hallway. I didn't know him. I didn't know what he was going to do, so I stood still. He hit me over the head with something metal, and I must have passed out."

"What! Button Hugenby?" Nicholas paced and mumbled with his teeth clinched.

"He has my father's horseshoe!" exclaimed Percival.

Marie continued, "The next thing I remembered was gasping for air as something pressed down against my face. I couldn't breathe! A pillow lifted off my head, and I saw Mr. Hugenby over me. He pressed the pillow back onto my face, and I stopped breathing." Marie explained her next moments as a ghost. She opened her eyes, and no one was in the room. She stood to walk, feeling different but with no pain. The lack of pain was a noticeable discomfort. Her reflection in the mirror was only a cloud; she couldn't see herself.

Nicholas paced the floor with a clenched jaw and fists. Percival sat dumbfounded; Button Hugenby was evil!

"I heard a scratch on my door and a meow, and I realized I could still feel frightening chills," she continued.

"Erie," responded Nicholas.

"Yes, it was," said Marie.

"No, Erie, my cat. He followed me everywhere as a kitten, and I finally named him after the road sign nearest me. Erie Street. Seems to fit well."

"Your cat's name is Erie?" asked Percival.

"Yes."

Marie explained the difficulties in opening doors because of the makeup of her hands; they had changed in such a way that gripping a doorknob was difficult, practically impossible. Doors shook and rattled if she tried to open them, spooking many guests. Finally, she let the calico cat into her room.

She also learned that if she filled her thoughts with the understanding of how another person lived and breathed, she could morph into that person. The only ones she had so far accomplished included the young boy and the maid.

"I have tried to get out of the hotel, but I can't. I can't go outside the hotel. It feels as if I'm suffocating sometimes. I'm thinking there has to be a way out. Every day, I look for a new way out. I'm stuck here, seeking justice, I suppose. Mr. Braham is stuck here too, seeking revenge."

"Mr. Braham, he's here? He's a ghost?" as Percival.

"You don't know? Yes, he's here. In this hotel. I'm sure you've seen him sneaking around—"

"What! He's here?"

"Yes, I'm afraid so. The murderer of your father is here in this hotel! He's a tall man with an evil twirl of a mustache."

20

The Truth About Ghosts

And so, Marie revealed the truth about Lyman Braham, but she didn't reveal everything about herself, sensibly.

Marie, understandably, was a good woman. Truly, she was a kind and compassionate human just as she was as a ghost; with Percival, she didn't share everything.

Although a relatively trivial point, she didn't share how she was married, and how her husband Julien de Plenron lived with her in her parents' home de Chadoir. He wasted his late parents' inheritance, a small fortune of less than a year's worth of wages. Julien had a gift of creating poetic dreams and conveying them to Marie in the most romantic ways. He stirred her dreams to go up and far away.

Reality, however, kept her shoulders drawn and her head low. It showed itself as beads of sweat onto Marie's face and neck as she worked continuously throughout each day on the community's sick. Eventually, customers dwindled; they refused to "ever go into that house again" based on Julien's grumpy mood and snappy attitude at patients' arrivals into the home. He typically said nothing, and he always wore a scowl on his face. He made the atmosphere unwelcoming, even for Marie.

When they learned of a mighty ship boarding hundreds of passengers to the United States, and after Marie's parents never awoke from their sleep, Julien promised Marie a new life. He booked two third-class tickets, discounted for boarding as part of the medical team.

As they packed, Marie admitted to Julien, "Perhaps the open-space of a new country might place us on two different journeys." He stared without a word. She continued to pack the chest without looking up.

Once aboard the ship, Marie worked endlessly. Many passengers reported seasickness. She rarely saw Julien. He ventured away to social groupings, new connections, and new relationships. One of these new acquaintances was Mathew Dooley, a cafeteria worker. Julien found him to be entertaining and his Irish accent to be a jewel. Later and elsewhere, Julien met Lyman Braham, whose mustache kept a nest of beer foam. Lyman Braham claimed to be on the ship to flee from "a messy British investigation." Julien's friendship with Lyman brewed dangerously in one of the ship's pubs.

Mathew Dooley served Julien and Lyman many of their meals. On the third evening aboard the ship, Julien ate little.

He told Mathew he couldn't eat because of his difficult wife and loss of hope for his marriage.

Mathew, in hopes to cheer up the man, sat next to Julien, pulled a horseshoe out of his pocket, and placed it on the table. "Right here, ye' see, is me luck. 'Tis Irish luck! And me friend, ye must believe. Me home is in America with a beautiful wife because of it. Tis full of magic!" Mathew looked around him and placed the horseshoe back in his pocket. "It hung on me wall in Chicago. Did good for me 'n me wife. She's havin' a second boy soon. A boy, I just know! Me good boy Percival! We know, with the goodness of Holy Mary and the holy saints, the horseshoe promises good."

Julien listened and believed him. Later in the night, he expressed his belief in the Irish spirit, how it bore powerful Irish magic. He was attracted to magic, tokens, and luck. He shared with Lyman how it would be nice to have his own magic charm to swoon his wife back in love with him. Julien was a romantic in that way, in thought more than action. Lyman, in response, suggested they steal it.

The rest of Marie's account is filled in accurately, but it's not the full picture. Julien de Plenron, at the age of 35, disappeared the night the Titanic sank. It was the same night Lyman and Julien had plotted to steal Mathew's horseshoe. Marie never saw Julien again, and she never looked for him.

Ten years later, Marie arrived at the Blaughvoyon Hotel. She met the debonair owner and was smitten. She met his calico pet cat that lived in the hotel, usually staying close by its owner.

"The little thing seemed to have found me; it came straight for me ten years ago. It's been my Erie little cat since," Nicholas explained.

Marie shared her reason for being in Chicago, and it was her compassion for the Dooley family that hooked Nicholas to love her. Unfortunately, her death was pronounced as a natural death while sleeping in her hotel room. While he deemed it incredulous, Nicholas had no other explanation. Within days of her death and in his grief, Nicholas heard guests speaking of seeing a ghost. They described the ghost just as one would describe Marie. She'd never show her ghostly self to him, even after he searched for her on every floor each night. She remained hidden from him, but she allowed the cat to take tokens of her belongings to Nicholas. Of course, as romantic a gesture as this was, Nicholas wanted to see her. To hire a Dooley would turn the eyes of Marie to eventually—he hoped — show herself to Nicholas.

The hotel had an angrier pulse where Button Hugenby and Lyman Braham spent their time. The men — or the man and the evil ghost — were daily plagued with the terrors of the ghost Marie. Doors shook and slammed. Lights shut off. Items crashed and smashed to the ground. The men were in a state of fright, even the ghostly Lyman Braham. Lyman carried the horseshoe with him when he wandered the hotel. And he hung the horseshoe on the wall as not only Braham's trophy but as a shield of protection against Marie. Lyman, in particular, believed he needed its power to feel safe, refreshed, and alive, despite the obvious opposite. They daily felt like prey and pondered for a way to execute the ghost Marie. Lyman ordered Button to never touch the horseshoe.

Years later, in 1928, sixteen-year-old Percival Dooley placed his name on a hiring list at a table in downtown Chicago, just as Charlie, whose impatience with the ordeal festered, ordered Percival to do so. Nicholas Blaughvoyon earnestly scanned through the names and found "Percival Dooley, age 20," just what he'd been hoping and planning for several years. His hope rekindled. To hire a Dooley would turn the eyes of Marie to show herself to Nicholas. He shared his plan with Charlie over and over, igniting Charlie to make matters of Dooley employment come alive, so to speak. Nicholas shared his dream of how he and Marie could then continue in love, starting just where they left off six years ago when they first met. Nicholas approved the list of names for new employment, with Percival Dooley's name on top.

"See to it that this young man is given a job," he ordered the hiring group. "I strongly suggest you give him charge to attend to the V. Nolan." Nicholas gave his command just before leaving for his business trip to Paris.

Dooley, ... Lyman pondered the name on a new-employee list one day. It wouldn't leave his ghostly brain. He shared the story of the "wretched Irish beggar" with Button, being certain the dead man was from Chicago.

"Is it the same Dooley? Perhaps his son?" Button asked.

"It is possible," answered Lyman. "There can't possibly be more than one bloody Irishman named Dooley in Chicago."

The two men sat quietly and stared out the penthouse window at the view. Could Percival Dooley be the perfect bait to destroy Marie? They had a difficult thought to reason, for having Percival in the hotel could be a reward or a curse. The notion of conjuring an evil plan swelled their pride and their wicked smiles.

Button agreed and concluded that this hire would require quick action. The two men would pose as owners of the Blaughvoyon Hotel. Lyman was concerned about his mustache appearing unprofessional, but he agreed to play the part of Mr. Blaughvoyon.

"What do young Irish boys know about looking professional?" Button assured Lyman.

Lyman, aware of the slow renovation being done on Floor 24, repositioned everything to convince the new employee. Meanwhile, Button secured the secret by hiring guards and doorkeepers for Floor 24. He even hired a secretary.

They were ready. They confirmed to see that this Dooley never came near their horseshoe, perhaps by some unfortunate accident, similar to his father. Perhaps in an elevator. They conjured a plan for the new Dooley employee and the ghost Marie to destroy one another. They practiced foul-play and disassembled brackets and cords within the shaft of an elevator. It crashed on Percival Dooley's first week of work, earlier than expected.

But they claimed, even to themselves, that upon meeting Percival in the penthouse, they forgot they had left the horseshoe hanging on the wall. When they saw him gaze upon it, they knew he was Percival Dooley, son of Mathew Dooley, indeed.

21

The Horseshoe

It's not that Percival was too ill-equipped for such a dangerous journey, albeit he was only sixteen and had no previous involvement with ghosts nor with a stolen keepsake belonging to his beloved late father.

It was just a horseshoe. A horseshoe.

Percival wondered about its lucky power throughout his life, even if it was an Irish superstition. Faith placed in a superstition creates a powerful superstition. All the absurdity happening now had to have been in connection with the power of the horseshoe. Percival believed in the horseshoe more than he believed in ghosts. It was a real horseshoe. To think the horseshoe didn't belong to his pap would have been absurd. And so, he deduced that its power and its magic were real. Only because of the horseshoe, Percival placed trust in the existence of ghosts. He was certain the horseshoe could have and should have kept his father alive. Instead, it kept a thief alive. This horseshoe was now not only Percival's but everyone's focus.

It was Rex's focus. Rex would go after it despite the danger. He often expressed that he had no reason to believe in danger. Things happened with either a good or bad result, but "danger is no guarantee," he'd say.

It was the real Mr. Nicholas Blaughvoyon's focus. He went after the horseshoe to impress Marie, an extra measure. Marie herself would most definitely help, but her help would be for Percival, not for Mr. Blaughvoyon. Mr. Blaughvoyon's endeavor was for Marie and ultimately for himself. If he weren't so kind, Percival would have disliked him.

Rex wandered the hotel with Luellen until he lost her. It was after midnight. The halls of the guest rooms were quiet. However, although dignified, lobbies, ballrooms, and lounges on the second, third, and fourth floors were louder and filled with guests. Exchanges became interesting, worth staring at for a hotel guest who knew nothing of ghosts, horseshoes, or falling. Rex crossed paths with Percival in the lobby, both lucky to meet at just the right time. Rex then strolled toward an unused elevator where an attendant stood in his blue suit. Rex stood in front of him and studied the attendant's suit. In the midst, Nicholas Blaughvoyon spotted Rex and his bushy Italian mustache. Rex naturally had a gift for stirring curiosity. Nicholas walked behind Rex to meet him. Rex stood at the elevator and glanced over at Nicholas.

"You must know me," Rex smoothed out. "Do I know you? Have we done business?"

The door opened, and Nicholas followed Rex onto the elevator, the only other elevator with a magnificent chandelier besides the V. Nolan.

"No, not that I recall—"

"Twenty-fourth floor, good man," interrupted Rex to the elevator attendant.

"The twenty-fourth?" Nicholas asked with a slight smile, as if pleasantly surprised. "That floor is closed to guests. Even to hotel attendants."

"Right, right, but I'm neither."

"Well, if you don't work here and you're not a guest, what are you doing here?"

Rex peered at Nicholas out of the corner of his eye. "Mister, it's nothing for you to worry about. I have an important possession on Floor 24, and I intend to get it back. Who are you?"

Nicholas held out his hand. "Nicholas Blaughvoyon, hotel owner." Rex shook his hand.

"Really?" Rex stared at him for a moment before introducing himself.

"Ah! The brother of my employee, Percival. Considering the floor is closed,' continued Nicholas, "may I be of service to you? I'm happy to retrieve the horseshoe for you."

"How do you know about this?" Rex questioned, facing him squarely. "Who are you, really?"

"I just finished engaging in a deep conversation with your young brother, and he obviously has many deep conversations to come. I'm your ally, Mr. Dooley."

As Nicholas fluffed out dutiful terms of upholding hotel protocols, safety rules and requirements, and impending dangers, Rex stared placidly, expressing a chuckle at the word "dangers."

"Ultimately, sir," Nicholas concluded, "I intend to find and take the horseshoe before you and give it to your brother."

"Why get in my way? Step aside. This is my journey."

"My duty is to serve you, and in my hotel, you must get out of my way."

"Nonsense! Now, tell me this, Mr. Blaughvoyon, any love involved in you racing against the rightful owner? Is love pushing you to grab the horseshoe before me?" Rex asked. Nicholas looked confused and off-guard. Rex was known for believing that all senseless actions rooted from love. He asked again, "Is this persistence involving love?"

"Well..." Nicholas cleared his throat and glanced down, blushing. "And, yes, snatching the treasure would turn the pretty head of a particular pretty lady." Rex huffed an open-mouth laugh framed with a bushy mustache.

"Dear attendant," started Rex, "I changed me mind. The fourteenth floor, please."

Mr. Blaughvoyon looked bewildered. Did this early stop have anything to do with his beloved Marie?

Marie, the "particular lady" Nicholas spoke of, wanted something different from the two men. She lurked to find Lyman and Button, because vengeance lurked in the crevices of her plight for justice. Darkness crept in. She hunted for them; they were the only two she mindfully haunted in the years of her ghostly death, stuck in the Blaughvoyon Hotel.

22

The Depths of the Hotel

Percival and Rex experienced a lucky moment of crossing paths in the hotel lobby, as Percival had hoped. It happened just before Rex and Nicholas's cordial introductions and sharing of the elevator with the chandelier. And it started with Button Hugenby.

When Button wobbled, it looked like he had a conscience, as if his goodness (if there truly was any) pushed him back from taking the bad path. His own body pushed his own body back. So, he wobbled. He wobbled through Nicholas Blaughvoyon's office door and immediately asserted, "Permission to fire Percival Dooley, sir!" Apparently, he didn't yet know that his secret of murder was out.

"Mr. Blaughvoyon is looking for you, Button," responded Charlie. "Stick around. He'll be back."

"Why would he be looking for me?"

"Stick around," restated Charlie, halfway sitting on the corner of Nicholas's desk.

"I, uh, unfortunately, I can't stay," Button said as he backed up to the door and opened it. "I'm very busy-"

"Mr. Hugenby, sir!" Percival called out from the lobby. Beside him was Rex, glaring at Button. Rex strolled away, as inconspicuously as was capable for Rex to do, which was very little. "Please," continued Percival to Button Hugenby, "can we speak?"

"Ah, of course, dear boy," chimed Button. He didn't know Rex. He waved farewell to Charlie and approached Percival. Closer to him, Button lowered his voice: "What!"

Percival exchanged in an even lower voice, "Sir, I think they're after you." He motioned for Button to step into an elevator, several elevator doors away from Rex. As the automatic door closed, the two of them faced one another. Button wrinkled his eyebrows and allowed a long-standing formation of cigarette ashes to fall to the floor.

"The ghost! She, uh, she plans to kill you!" said Percival. Earlier, Percival conjured up a mess of a plan as he walked to find Button and luckily bumped into Rex. How to execute the plan was gradually clearing from a blur, albeit still blurry.

Button gave one long blink and insisted, "What happened?"

Percival elaborated on a dangerous "near-death" encounter with the "evil ghost woman." He pressed the button for Floor 24. "We gotta tell Mr. Blaughvoyon right away! He's in the penthouse?"

Button continued to stare at Percival because what Button knew was that Percival met the real Nicholas Blaughvoyon. What Button was uncertain of was who Percival believed, Button or Nicholas; but sensibility, even for an Irish boy, erred on the side of Nicholas. Button narrowed his eyes to give Percival a threatening message, as piercing as eyes could form. "They got to you, didn't they!"

Percival answered quickly, "I did what you said; I didn't believe a word!"

Like all sixteen-year-olds, Percival could see suspicion; sixteen-year-olds were commonly under suspicion, so they had practice in knowing it when they saw it, and Percival could see it.

The elevator dinged, and the door slid open automatically to Floor 24. He was getting closer to the horseshoe. He followed Button off the elevator.

"All falsehoods and lies, I am certain. Preposterous!" shouted Button.

"And the man downstairs, if he's not the real Mr. Blaughvoyon, who is he?" Percival asked, engaging in terrible conversation. Before Percival took another step, Button slammed Percival against the hallway wall with his chubby hand around Percival's throat.

"If, Dooley?" shook Button's voice. "I won't stand here and be questioned by an Irish low-down elevator boy!"

As Percival managed a weak punch to Button's jaw, a man's voice down the hall sounded: "Mr. Hugenby?"

Button released Percival and gave his jaw a slight rub as he obliged the voice. A guard was hesitant but finally allowed Button and Percival into the penthouse lobby. Percival dreaded the next moments of that late night. He wondered where Rex was. Luellen was not at the desk. Button opened the penthouse door, allowing Percival to enter.

"Lyman!" Button shouted. Button didn't call for Mr. Blaughvoyon, Percival noticed. What a nasty feeling to be in the same room with the murderer of his father, to hear the man's name aloud! The short Indian man swept up broken glass, mumbling loudly toward Percival. With a deep breath, Percival stomped straight to the wall where the horseshoe still hung. Percival gazed upon its worthiness for too long.

"That's mine!" demanded Lyman, standing behind him. Percival recognized his voice to be like a trumpet announcing war on a battlefield. Lyman elongated his arm and wrapped his long fingers around one end of the horseshoe. Percival held the other end tight.

"It's me Pap's. Let go!" Percival shouted.

"He knows things, Button," said Lyman. He then enunciated, "You mean that hideous Irish man with the pathetic kitten on that blasted boat?"

"Kitten?" Percival repeated. Behind him, the Indian man slid open the glass door. With that, Lyman let go of his pulling of the horseshoe as Percival continued pulling. Percival shot backwards onto the balcony and tried to steady his confused feet.

"He caught the likens of that pathetic woman who left her husband to drown." Lyman gave Percival a shove to his chest, and normally this shouldn't have mattered; balconies on twenty-fourth floors have railings to stop falls. Percival should have had a safety net. However, the falls of Percival Dooley were designed with a decline. Fittingly, the renovation left an uncompleted railing for the balcony. Percival's body did not stop on the balcony but fell to depths and depths of black night air. The mumbling Indian man slid shut the door and locked it. Lyman now had pushed two Dooley men to their demise.

Here is where the life of Percival should have ended, or anyone else's life in a similar predicament. But Percival had four advantages this time. First, Percival had the horseshoe, and it will soon reveal its favor. He had a second advantage established in his life: this was not the first time Percival had fallen off a high-rise balcony; he had experience. His instincts were now prepared. Third, love for his Pap roared mightily, and failure was no option. Lastly (and the most noticeable of all advantages), Percival was more likely to survive falls more than any type of danger he faced. Dooley logic should have owned the belief that Percival was at his safest in life when falling. But he was a smart sixteen-year-old; he was bound to die at the next fall. Or, the next fall.

As he fell backward, in Percival's tight grip, the horseshoe locked onto one of the old rail poles just as he fell back off the balcony. He gripped each side of the horseshoe, and he felt his shoulders stretch and tear as his body dangled heavy, dependent on a horseshoe. The pole bent and continued to bend until it bended completely forward. Percival grabbed the pole. His face was inches away from the loosened bolts in the cement floor. Inside the penthouse, he saw the shoes of Button and Lyman leaving. Percival felt woozy and his sight blackened. Once again, here is where the life of Percival should have ended. But someone must have been catching Percival, for with each fall, having no safety precautions in place and, of course, no suspicions of falling again, he survived. The balcony seemed to lift him back to the floor, like the hotel's hand. Back on his feet, he pounded on the glass with the horseshoe until it shattered. And it gave way easily, like a sacrificial encouragement from the hotel itself

23

Cat Scratches

The pandemonium in the Blaughvoyon Hotel swirled and swirled on several floors. It could have caused a cyclone if the hotel wasn't so careful to stand absolutely still. Standing in an elevator on the fourteenth floor were Rex and Nicholas. Stumbling through a penthouse of broken glass on the twenty-fourth floor was Percival. The whereabouts of Button and Lyman were uncertain, and Marie couldn't have been far behind the wicked pair. Her revenge stirred on this night more than ever before.

The cat was not in the hotel at the time. It sat on the windowsill of the Dooley home, staring at Lena and scratching the window.

Percival walked away from the penthouse down the dark hallway. His heart could not calm down, and he was grieving.

His father was dead, drowned alone at the bottom of the unforgiving ocean. "Me Pap," he whispered. He thought of telling Lena that her husband was never coming home. Percival fell to his knees in defeat beside an elevator door. His clothes were torn; his shoulder burned and felt misplaced; his left sleeve was almost gone, and he had a scratch on his arm which he couldn't recall its initial appearance. His face throbbed with pain. He was glad of it. The throb understood how he felt.

He heard footsteps behind him.

"You're fired," Button Hugenby shouted, "and I must confiscate the stolen item of the horseshoe, at once. You stole it. Hand it here."

Percival stammered to his feet with eyebrows and lips more wrinkled in disgust than Button ever portrayed.

Lyman stammered down the hallway so quickly that his speed didn't match the movement of his long legs. Here was the murderer of Percival's father, and Percival didn't know what to do. Button chuckled a low trill as if he found the moment pleasant.

"Marie-Louise Chadoir told me everything," managed Percival.

"Ah, I had forgotten the dame's name," Button claimed. "She's still floating around here somewhere because you never fulfilled your duty to catch her."

Both Lyman and Button charged toward Percival. In the painful tugging, pressing, and pulling with punches plunged into Percival's stomach and face, Percival gasped for breath and realized fights, too, just like falls, he has survived. He gripped the horseshoe tight.

Lyman pried open the elevator door to empty dark space. "Once you finally die, I'll get it back!" he shouted, and he again shoved Percival toward the empty shaft. Percival looked down the shaft and saw the rooftop of an elevator, stationary ten floors below. Percival grabbed hold of the side of the door and stopped himself, but he dropped the horseshoe. A definite thud announced its arrival to the elevator far below. Also, hearing the horseshoe's thud were the elevator's interior guests: Rex, Nicholas, and the elevator attendant. They exchanged puzzled expressions.

The attendant exclaimed, "No union savin' me outta here!" He opened the door and ran into the Floor 14 hallway. Rex and Nicholas remained inside. With the door still ajar, Rex pulled out a horseshoe given to him by Percival. The horseshoe came from Lena's hope chest. It sparked an idea in Percival, so he took it.

"You have the horseshoe, sir?" asked Nicholas. "What are you doing?"

"Mr. Blaughvoyon, your employee Percival Dooley has a plan," answered Rex. "I don't know it yet myself." Nicholas stared at the horseshoe with interest. Scratches covered the horseshoe, and he pondered its meaning.

Scratches led Nicholas there, in the elevator where he stood. Cat scratches had led him since 1918. He noticed the first cat scratch on a hotel door, Floor 14, Room 1471. The next scratch was a shred in a pillowcase reported to him by housekeeping after the body of Marie-Louise was found. Her own arm carried a slight scratch. And the fourth scratch kept his full attention to this day. The back of Button Hugenby's hand, when he was promoted to be manager, had two deep scratches that formed an "X" in a dark red scab.

"Just a mean cat," Button explained. But the scratching continued, building Nicholas's curiosity. Each door on each floor of the crashed elevator carried an "X," etched in by the claws of a cat.

As Nicholas stepped outside the elevator, he wondered, *Where is my Erie cat? And where is Marie?*

Ten floors up, Percival stared at his father's horseshoe, lying on the elevator's roof.

"Get it back, Percival!" shouted Marie's low voice. The men turned to see her backing away from them toward the stairwell.

Lyman turned back to Percival with a smile and said, "Yes, indeed! Jump, you coward!" Marie disappeared behind the stairwell door. Button and Lyman hurried after her. Percival continued to stare at the horseshoe. If he didn't jump, they would get the horseshoe. If he did jump, he would die, and they would get the horseshoe. He couldn't move. The elevator didn't move either. He also realized it wasn't the horseshoe he'd jump for as much as it was his Pap. Then, he pushed reason aside, and he jumped. But at least this time, he didn't fall.

He had ten floors to descend. The moment his foot detached from Floor 24, he thought for a second of something nearby to grab, but there was nothing. A couple of floors down, panic struck. And then, the strangest falling moment happened, like something Percival had never experienced. His falling slowed down. It slowed down so much he had a moment to analyze the feather-like float. Either his body was sinking as if in a grand mass of water, or the hotel was sinking to lighten his landing. The landing was forceful but survivable. He grabbed the horseshoe and held it close to his chest.

Suddenly, the elevator lowered slightly and stopped, exposing Percival to Floor 14. He rolled off onto the hallway floor.

Percival met eyes with Rex, who was still in the elevator with Nicholas. Rex and Nicholas leveled the elevator back to the floor. Lyman and Button stormed toward Percival as he scurried into the elevator and grabbed the key from the elevator wall.

"Give me my horseshoe! How are you still alive? Are you dead now, too?" Lyman shouted.

"I don't have it," Percival answered. "Must still be on the roof."

Something suddenly brought a smile to Lyman's face. He stared at the chandelier, where a horseshoe was hooked onto it. Slowly, he walked into the elevator, not noticing the others running out. He reached up and began trying to unhook the horseshoe. As he did, Marie appeared and, frantically and with a roar, closed the gate and the door of the elevator with all her ghostly might. Lyman now couldn't be seen, but those in the hallway could hear him. He let out a growl, demanding to be let out. A mix of silence and chilling screeches and bangs caused the elevator to shake. Each boom caused chills to surface on Percival's body. The commotion sounded too violent to be only one person. How did the elevator remain still and suspended? It was in the hands — the tight, angry grip — of the hotel. The sound was haunting enough for everyone to back up. After some time, only silence remained.

Nicholas, unlike his hesitant comrades, pulled open the door. Inside, the walls suffered with indentions and scratches. The handrail was completely torn off the wall and broken. The extensive damage, though, was a victory!

Lyman Braham was gone, eaten by the hotel, never to return to the living realm again.

Percival was relieved until he witnessed the embracing between his beloved Marie and Nicholas Blaughvoyon.

24

Closures

Hotels pride themselves on carrying rows of doors. Symbols for new beginnings and endings. Each door opened, closed, locked, kept out, invited in, showed dark unseen things, and a dare to step in. Such a door waited for Marie. After parting a long, loving goodbye with Nicholas, she walked past Button Hugenby, being held in a tight armlock by Charlie.

"Thanks, Charlie," she said. Charlie gave a cordial nod. She now walked toward Percival, and Percival stared, basking in bliss. Her love for Nicholas, her death and ghostly life, and the age gap didn't matter and didn't stop Percival's feelings for her.

"I'm in love with you," confessed Percival as Nicholas and Rex watched him in his vulnerability.

What followed was the first recorded time ever of a ghost blushing.

"Well, I'm much older and I'm not living. Love is in life. Not death." Marie responded.

"But I still think I might be. I am. And I love me Pap, and he's ... not living. I love him." And he found the truth. Reality. Love continued living amidst death.

Marie asked about his plans for the horseshoe.

"Whatever me Mum wants to do with it, I think," he answered. He had more work to do, but Marie's work was done. Percival stared at Marie and felt a tear come to visit. He looked down at the horseshoe. It felt warm and alive. It fit in his hand as if it was glad to be back home. When he glanced up again, Marie was gone. A door around the corner sounded a cordial shut, and light seeping through the crack of the doorway shut off.

Heavy tightness filled Percival's chest.

With his low, Dooley voice, he repeated, "Marie-Louise, I love you."

A thousand thoughts of his father swirled in a thousand different directions, and he cried. The air was lighter. And full, too, for the whole purpose of enveloping this moment they received answers and closure together. They stood still, and no one said so, but they each thought they heard something to the liking of a rhythmic thrumming of pipes with a steady vibration under their feet. Like a heartbeat. Undoubtedly, they stood in the core of the hotel's heart.

Traps were temporary. Vast expanses give freedom to die in, like the vast expanse of the ocean. In freedom, Mathew

Dooley died. In freedom of a new open door, Marie left the hotel.

Percival thought of his mother.

Rex strolled down the hallway alone. At a distance he stopped and leaned against the wall, hanging his head. No one spoke. No one moved. Finally, Rex returned.

Percival noticed the broken heart of Nicholas worn on his face. Nicholas stood still in uncertainty. Rex strolled closer to Nicholas and quietly spoke.

"Mr. Blaughvoyon. Rex for short. A nasty day for us." His voice dragged in melancholy. "But you're lucky, too. You need a new manager, and I'm open to accepting the job."

Nicholas shook back into his significant role as a CEO, and he spoke with authority over the sickly hotel, finding the germ: "Button Hugenby, a murderer! A cold-blooded killer! You'll never step even a thought in my hotel again. You're not only fired, you will find authority waiting for you just outside the back employee doors. They are here to arrest you for the murder of Marie-Louise Chadoir. Other mysteries of the hotel are also being investigated, and I imagine you're the culprit. Either way, I'll see to it that you rot. Off you go."

"Sir," Button began with the strangest condescending look to Mr. Blaughvoyon, "with the Union, I have defense attorneys at my disposal—"

A long, low meow interrupted Button's insults; the meow's source unseen. Button cleared his throat and continued, "And if the Union doesn't destroy you, the stock market will."

Button Hugenby tried to escape down the steps to the bottom floor. At the back door, Erie prowled from the darkness close to Button. Button paused. The cat stared wide-eyed at Button and moaned and growled with such a low voice that the air trembled. Button, wanting to escape the ominous hotel spot, opened the back door to find arresting officers. He stumbled and fell down the quick descent of steps. It was a weak fall, incomparable to what Percival knew about falls. It was a weak fall.

Percival's shoulders and his face drooped with exhaustion. How he had wanted to carry the horseshoe triumphantly. He imagined his mother's face upon beholding the horseshoe. He imagined her tears despite a feeling of completion from what she'd wondered for years. She'd soon have knowledge that would break her heart. Percival had nothing, and today, he would go home like any other day, with nothing more. But he wouldn't continue to see his mother's puffy eyes glare out the window as if maybe this time she'd see Mathew. No, nothing. She'd look back down and try to continue her life, wondering if maybe he'd be home in a minute. An upcoming miserable moment would soon replace her current misery.

25

Beloved

Percival and Rex walked home under the beams of street-lights. To the clutter of mazes of homes, the puddles of mud, the stares. His new work shoes collected dust and dirt, and he was happy for it.

He opened the door into the kitchen, where Lena sat, smiling sadly.

"Oh, me boys!" she spoke in her low voice. "If your Pap could see ya' now." Rex treated the top of her head with a kiss. She made no comment on Percival's discolored face and torn shirt.

"Ah, dear Mum," Percival began, and Mrs. Dooley interrupted him a million times before he brought out the horseshoe for her to see. She was then quiet and still as she stared at it. Percival placed the horseshoe in her hands. She embraced it, breathed in deep and out with crying and kisses for the horseshoe. Percival shared the truth of her beloved's death, her beloved's whereabouts. She stood and turned her back to her sons. In all the years of wishing and hoping, she kept a sternness, a loud strength. It was who she was. Her face changed now, and as the sternness abandoned her, the Dooley sons couldn't see the broken Lena Dooley.

Percival, Rex, and Mum shared the time of brokenness. It was inescapable. They passed the horseshoe, each one welled with tears upon admiring it in their hands. They wept and laughed and shared how Pap would have really handled things at the hotel, "with a crack o' the hid, I tell ya' that!" Mrs. Dooley exclaimed.

Mrs. Dooley tried to brighten the moment, but each time she did, a frown overcame her.

They shared crying moments with no words, a loss best explained by seeing only the white space on the paper.

"Mum, no big ship killed Pap," offered Percival. "He was murdered."

Lena moaned and Rex growled. "They were all murdered by others and not a ship, in one way or the other."

"We're all murdered, aren't we!" exploded Lena. "The whole lot of us!" Each conversation snippet trailed into more silence.

Percival thought about Lyman Braham, but stayed quiet about it. He realized Lyman died by falling. Percival fell many times and lived. Then, Lyman ultimately perished in an elevator. Percival cunningly (he thought to himself, and somewhat accurately) survived his dangerous elevator experiences. Lyman was a weakling, and Percival felt mighty.

And he felt love. He had the vivid memory of Marie. Percival lengthened his upper body to sit up straight.

"Did me Mathew tell the lady anything about me?" She smiled big at Percival with her puffy face, beady tear-soaked eyes, and crooked teeth. "Do ya' know, Percy?" Her frown returned, and so did the cry. "Did he say anything about his love for me? What else did he say, Percy?"

"Yes, Mum! 'Tis why Marie came to Chicago! To find you, Mum! Pap's love for you, it touched her, and she knew you needed to know. She knew Pap loved you. He loved you so much, Mum!"

Percival thought hard about what else Marie told him: "He wanted you to know that he died ... romantically? Breathing in the forbidden. His words, Mum. Not mine. But that's what he told Marie. That's what he wanted you to know."

"Ah! Such a poetic man, me Mathew!" Lena sighed deeply. Love proved its strength the most in the most despairing of times. It weakened sadness and anger before it could root. Lena, for the first moment since being told of Mathew's death, looked content. "Another realm. He always spoke of the luck of another realm."

"Yes!" Rex responded. "For Percy, the Blaughvoyon Hotel!"

"What? What's that, Mum?"

"Realm, Percy," Lena answered. "Something your pap said. And ya' Pap blasted told me it wasn't the whiskey. But 'twas a place, somewhere." She held the horseshoe in front of her face and said, "Perhaps all these years, he's been back in our own realm. With us."

26

Eastward

Hubert helped Percival plan a bus trip to the eastern coast.

"You won't be close enough to my hometown, but that's okay. If' ya' see a Downey, tell'm I said hello." The Dooleys decided to travel in a straight line going east until they hit the ocean. They planned for their stop to be Westport, Massachusetts. This distance was all they had money for, and it practically made a straight line from Chicago to Westport, straight across the states. Mr. Blaughvoyon agreed to give Percival an advance in payment plus a bonus for assurance that Percival wouldn't file a lawsuit against the hotel. At the end of the day, Nicholas Blaughvoyon was a businessman. One of the most successful businessmen in the world.

"Any Downey family wanna take us in for a night or two?" Percival asked Hubert.

"My family's in Jersey, yeah. And no offense, Percy, but they ain't lettin' no Irish people in their house. I'm sorry, my friend. They don't know you like I do, okay?"

Before Percival was offended, he heard a greeting behind him.

"Hi ya', Dooley." Charlie stood tall with almost a full smile on his face.

"Sir, thank you," Percival said, extending his hand.

Charlie looked confused before shaking his hand. "For what, kid?"

"You sought me out when I didn't know I needed to be found. It made all the difference." Percival surprised himself with such a statement.

"I'm always here for ya'," Charlie answered with a look of admiration toward Percival. "Take your trip and come back to work."

From bus station to bus station, Percy, Rex, and Mrs. Dooley traveled east. If Mrs. Dooley saw the sun to the right or left of the bus, she'd shout to the driver, "Excuse me, are we still east?" She also asked several times, "Whose got the horseshoe? You remembered the horseshoe, didn't ya', boys?" They also had a couple of delays that gave them time to eat and wait in the bus stations. In Westport, they walked to the ocean from the bus station.

The massive expanse of the ocean was difficult to grasp. A wind from the ocean caused them to all take off their hats. Rex and Percival helped their mother through the rocky shore to meet their feet with the end of the water.

"The last time me saw this ocean, I was wed to your father. We came over in 1899." She stared out and laughed a bit. "We had a time, the two of us!" She stood on a nearby boulder. "Mathew!" she shouted. "Mathew Dooley, it's your beloved and trothed!" She cried for a slight moment and regained her composure. "It's Lena, me love. We found your horseshoe, and we're here to give it back to ya', because Mathew, I am sorry, so sorry you don't have it. And me loves you!

"For thy sweet love remembered such wealth brings,
That then I scorn to change my state with kings.
So, now you rest." She stared out at the ocean for a moment. Lena memorized the couplet from Shakespeare, hoping to recite it to Mathew when he returned home.

Percival had the horseshoe and climbed the boulder with his mother to throw the horseshoe out into the deep.

"Love ya', Paps," Percival and Rex shouted. Percival reared back, and it's possible that Percival hadn't practiced throwing for some time, for the horseshoe landed on another rock a few yards out. Lena and Rex glare at Percival.

"An eejit! A blasted eejit!" Lena proclaimed.

"'Tis why you fall. Your weak arms. You can't catch ya'self!" Rex argued.

"Alright! I'm no Cubs pitcher, now am I? Maybe I'm like Pap. Could he play sports?" Percival tried to defend himself.

"Better than you. 'Twas downright embarrassing," Lena said.

"Have you ever in your life thrown anything?" Rex continued.

"I'll try again. Let me."

Both Rex and Lena interrupted him with objections. Rex recovered the horseshoe and walked out further. He stood for a moment, ankle-deep in the water. He stared down at the horseshoe and just as he reared back to throw it, Percival shouted, "Love you, Pap!" Rex turned around at Percival.

"You're trying to throw me off, ain't ya'!"

"I'm sorry," Percival answered.

"Shuttup, Percy!" Lena exclaimed. Rex reared back his arm, and Lena shouted, "Wait! Don't throw it!" Rex turned around toward Lena in confusion.

"Come back this way, Rex. Bring it to me."

Upon giving the horseshoe to Lena, Rex asked, "You want to throw it yourself, Mum?"

"No, I'm not throwing it. I've decided to keep it." Rex and Percival stare at their mother.

"I have a feeling me Mathew wants me to keep it." They looked out at the deep waters as if searching for confirmation. Staring at the ocean anymore gave them a cold, dull feeling. They embraced one another.

"There," Lena replied. "I want to go home." Her sons felt the same need. Lena held the horseshoe, and they sat on a boulder for a rest as they thought of home.

Particularly Percy. He had an extraordinary craving for some potato cakes. He hadn't enjoyed one in ages.

27

Misfortune

And to what do we owe the calico cat? It gave its share of placid "meows" which were typically ignored by most. Although Mr. Blaughvoyon found the cat in Chicago, the old cat's life began in Ireland.

A little over sixteen years earlier, Mathew arrived in his Irish hometown village of Kilmurry to share love and a good-bye with his mother days before she died. In his mourning, he spent a few days in her cottage, settling matters of possessions and finding places of his roots. He stood in front of the old Carroll's pub, where he walked in and met the love of his life. He walked the dirt road where he often rode his bike with his books in the basket. Meanwhile, Mathew's cousins helped Mathew secure a crewman job on a passenger ship bound for America. He thanked them with a promise to bring his family back to Kilmurry soon.

Amid the sorrow of losing his mother, he quickly packed for his home in Chicago. The White Star Line supervisor instructed Mathew to report to Queenstown before dawn on the day of departure. Aboard a carriage, he left Kilmurry on a Wednesday, the day before the ship's departure. On the countless miles down a dirt road to Queenstown, between the vast green fields, a hard rain started and pounded around them. Visibility was difficult, and the horses struggled to keep the wheels rolling in the muck. Through the rain, Mathew narrowed his eyes at a spot beside the road.

"What is that? A creature, I think," Matthew shared. A small kitten balled itself up beside the road. It didn't scurry as the carriage approached.

"Why, it's still there!" declared the coachman. "It was in the same place just yesterday."

The kitten's life began just east of Kilmurry by falling off a ledge away from its mother. It tired from searching for its family, and the exhausted creature finally settled beside the roadway.

"Please, stop a moment!" shouted Mathew. He climbed out of the carriage and bent down in the rain for a better view of the newly born kitten. It was the love he needed at that moment. He warmed the kitten in his coat and fed it some bread. Unwilling to abandon it, he brought it aboard the Titanic, unseen for a while. Upon seeing the cat, the crewman teased Mathew by holding the poor kitten over the guardrail, exposed to the ocean. In their quarters, the kitten got kicked out of the way more than once. Mathew took care of the calico kitten and expressed to many aboard the ship it was a gift to his family in Chicago.

Aboard the Titanic, Mathew found a balcony on one of the top floors of the ship, accessible only by crewmen. At this great height (one of many heights for the kitten), overlooking the wrinkled expanse of the sea, the hearts of Mathew and his dear kitten knit together.

"For thy sweet love remembered such wealth brings," Mathew recited the love sonnet, "That then I scorn to change my state with kings." Devotion between the man and the cat sealed, and Mathew held the kitten close.

The Titanic carried several pets, including birds, dogs, and cats. Several eyewitnesses claimed to see a tiny baby calico kitten among the Titanic survivors at Pier 54 port in New York City. It pranced deeper into the mainland heading east, and finally at varied heights within the Blaughvoyon Hotel.

Although Mr. Blaughvoyon named the cat Erie, this wasn't its original name. Years before, upon all the trials the poor kitten endured, Mathew shook his head with a smile and named the calico kitten Misfortune.

Thank you for reading *Percival Dooley*! Please leave a review
and thank you for supporting indie authors.

For more fiction from the early twentieth century, enjoy K.C. Foster's historical romance,
Heather's Journey.
Found at all online retailers.